UP THE CREEK!

KEVIN MILLER

MILLSTONE
PRESS

Kevin Miller/Millstone Press
Box 380
Kimberley, BC, Canada V1A 2Y9

www.millstonepress.ca
www.facebook.com/MilliganCreekSeries

Up the Creek!/Kevin Miller. -- 1st ed.
ISBN-13: 978-1519253262/10: 1519253265

Cover illustration by Kierston Vande Kraats (https://kvdk.carbonmade.com)

Author photo by Huw Miller.

Dedication

For Victor, who accompanied me down the real Milligan Creek and on so many other adventures, and for Mom, who was the first to brave those frigid waters.

Contents

1

THE FIRST BOOTFUL

"On your mark, get set, go!"

Thirteen-year-old Chad Taylor waved his scarf in the air as his younger brother, Matt, and their friend, Dean Muller, raced to the edge of the gravel country road. They each grabbed a gray stick off the ground, tossed it into the water that rushed through the pair of aluminum culverts that passed beneath the road, and then dashed back to the other side.

"Beat ya!" Matt said, raising his arms in triumph.

"Not yet you haven't. Watch." Dean put his cap on backwards, lay down on a culvert, and peered at the water below. "There it is!" He pointed to his stick as it sailed through ahead of Matt's. "I beat you!"

"That's not your stick. Yours was the short one," Matt protested.

"Yeah right."

"I'm serious."

Chad shook his head and smiled at his brother. "Just admit you lost, Matt."

"Yeah," Dean added.

"All right, all right, you got me. Let's do it again," Matt said, already searching the ground for more sticks.

Dean checked his watch. "I don't think so. I should be getting home."

"Come on, Dean," Matt said. "Your mom won't mind if you're a few minutes late for supper."

"That's what you said last time. And I got grounded from TV for a week."

"That's because you didn't make it home until after ten o'clock."

"Because you left him stuck up on a roof with no way to get down," Chad reminded him.

"In the rain," Dean added.

"How did I know you were waiting for me to help you get down?"

"Because you had the ladder."

Matt smiled sheepishly. "Oh yeah. Well, we can't worry about that right now. There's too much to do. The snow is melting like crazy, and we haven't even gotten a bootful yet."

Just then, something in the water caught Chad's eye. "Hey look, a whirlpool!"

Matt and Dean ran over to the edge of the road. Sure enough, a small whirlpool had formed between the two culverts. It sucked small sticks, straw, and other debris down into the cold, dark water.

Matt grabbed a larger stick off the side of the road and tossed it into the water. It inched toward the whirlpool and then turned on its end before it was sucked down into the blackness.

Dean shivered. "I'd hate to get caught in that."

"Yeah, if you were an ant," Matt replied, punching Dean playfully in the shoulder.

"Or a frog," Chad said, punching Dean from the other side.

"Hey, knock it off!" Dean swiped at Matt, but he

ducked out of the way, laughing. Dean gave Chad a friendly shove instead.

Chad regained his footing and then looked out at the ribbon of water that flowed out of the muddy fields. "The water sure is high this year."

What was normally a dry grassy ditch had become a full-fledged stream swollen with the runoff from the winter's unusually high snowfall. The stream glinted and sparkled in the fading sunlight as it flowed through a flooded clump of trees that were just starting to bud.

The boys picked up their bikes to head home.

"My dad says it hasn't peaked yet," Dean said. "Lots of snow in the bushes still hasn't melted."

"Hmm . . .." Matt stared at the water, a faraway look in his green eyes.

Dean swallowed hard. He had seen that look before—too many times. "What are you thinking, Matt?"

Matt looked at him and grinned wildly.

Chad laughed. "I think you'd better get home for supper, Dean—while you still can."

"Okay, see you guys tomorrow." Dean got on his bike and started pedaling.

"Not so fast, Dean. Just hear me out for a moment," Matt said.

Dean's shoulders sank as he glided to a stop. He knew Matt would not take no for an answer. "Just make it quick."

"Do you guys remember that TV show about whitewater rafting we watched a few weeks ago?"

"Not me. I was still grounded, remember?" Dean reminded him.

"Yeah, that looked wild," Chad replied. "I'd love to do something like that."

Dean shook his head. "You can count me out. Way

too dangerous."

"Aw, get off it, Dean," Matt said. "What could go wrong? They were wearing life jackets and helmets, and there's no way a raft like that could ever sink."

"That's what you think," Dean replied. "What if it ran into a tree or a rock? I'm sure people die every year doing that sort of thing."

Matt stared out at the reddish sun, which was just starting to dip toward the horizon. "Well, I don't think there'll be any danger of that happening on the trip we're going to take."

Dean eyed him suspiciously. "What do you mean *we*? What trip?"

Matt turned to his brother. "Chad, does Andrew still have that three-man rubber dinghy we used at the lake last summer?"

Andrew Loewen was a close companion of the boys. He lived on a farm a few miles away from the Taylors, who also lived on a farm about four miles outside of town.

Chad nodded. "Yeah, his dog bit a hole in it, but I think it could be patched."

"Good. We'll call him when we get home."

Matt got on his bike and started to pedal away. Chad followed.

"See you tomorrow Dean," Chad called back over his shoulder. He and Matt grinned at each other.

Dean stood there for a moment, a confused look on his freckled face. Then he looked toward his friends. "Wait a second. Why do you need a dinghy?" He turned back to the water, and his eyes went wide. "You're not going to try floating down here, are you? You'd get stuck in the culvert!"

"Not here, dummy," Matt said as he circled back to Dean. "On Milligan Creek. I bet the water is roaring through there."

Dean looked up. In the distance he saw the lights from the grain elevators in the town of Milligan Creek, Saskatchewan, where the boys went to school. Matt and Dean were in grade six, and Chad was in grade seven. The town took its name from the stream that flowed through it. The creek itself was named after the first family who settled in the area. Throughout most of the year, the creek was small and sluggish, but it was sure to reach record heights with the extra runoff.

"Well, you can count me out. I'm not getting in any flimsy boat and floating down a raging river," Dean said. "You'll probably get hung up on a beaver dam and sink."

"Suit yourself," Matt said, still circling on his bike. "Maybe you can stay on shore and be our safety manager."

Dean got on his bike. "Oh yeah? We'll see what your parents have to say about the idea." He started to pedal away, but his front wheel hit a huge rock.

"Hey, wait a second, I'm—"

Before he could get the words out, he flipped over his handlebars and tumbled down the ditch—right into the flowing water.

"Whoo-hoo! The first bootful!" Matt cried as he turned back to help his friend.

"First pantful, too!" Chad added.

Chad and Matt ditched their bikes and then climbed down to help Dean out of the stream. Once they dragged him and his bike back up onto the road, Dean sat down and tugged at his rubber boots.

"Agghh! They're stuck!"

"Here, let us help." Matt grabbed Dean's right boot, and Chad grabbed the left. Matt looked at Chad. "Ready? One, two, three—heave!" The boys pulled as hard as they could.

"Hey, careful, you're pinching my toes!"

Just then there was a loud sucking noise, and Dean's

right boot popped off, sending Matt stumbling backwards down the ditch—straight into the water. Chad nearly fell over with laughter as Matt coughed and spluttered.

A horn honked in the distance. They looked up as an old, blue pick-up truck pulled up. Chad recognized Andrew's tight, curly hair in the passenger window. He was with his dad, Fred. As soon as the truck came to a stop, Andrew jumped out.

"Hey guys, what's going on?"

Chad pointed at the stream where Matt was sloshing around trying to stand up. "It's the second bootful!"

Matt spluttered and puffed as he finally regained his footing.

Dean scanned the water. "Hey, where's my boot?"

Matt searched the water flowing around his legs. "I must have dropped it."

"Can't you see it?" Dean hopped on one foot toward the edge of the road for a better look.

Matt looked around again and then shook his head. "No. Current must have carried it off. Sorry, Dean. I'll replace it, but you can have one of mine 'til you get home, if you like."

He stood on one foot and tried to pull off his other boot. He hopped for a couple of steps before he fell back into the water.

Andrew slapped his forehead. "I can't believe that just happened."

Dean smiled despite himself. "Hey, quit fooling around, I have to get home. And wait 'til my mom hears about my boot."

Matt, who was completely drenched, grinned as he climbed back out of the water. He sat down on the grassy bank, pulled off his boot, and then turned it upside down. Water poured out of it.

"Here you go." He tossed it to Dean.

Dean grimaced as he held up the sopping wet boot. He winced as he squeezed his foot into it. "It's cold."

"Not nearly as cold as Milligan Creek is going to be when we raft it this weekend," Matt said as he hopped up the bank.

Andrew shot him a quizzical look. "What are you talking about?"

Matt put his arm around Andrew's shoulders. "If you give us a ride home, I'll tell you all about it."

Andrew turned to his dad. Mr. Loewen looked Matt up and down and then jabbed his thumb at the truck box.

"That's okay with me, but you're riding in the back, Aquaboy."

Matt jammed his sopping wet cap over his thick blonde hair. "You ain't seen nothin' yet."

Dean rolled his eyes. "Here he goes."

The other boys laughed as they helped Mr. Loewen load their bikes into the back of the truck.

2

A New Plan

The next day after school, Matt, Chad, Dean, and Andrew raced to Milligan Creek on their bikes. They skidded to a halt on the old, rusted bridge next to the graveyard. Matt got there first, as usual. He jumped off his bike and ran to the edge of the bridge.

"Awesome. Look at all that water!"

The swollen creek had risen so much overnight that barely three feet remained between the water and the bridge.

Chad stood beside his brother. "Wow, if a big tree swept through here, it would wipe the bridge right out."

Dean, who was about to step onto the bridge, thought better of it and remained on the road.

Andrew studied the water. "I've got bad news though. You'll never get down that with a rubber dinghy."

Matt stepped back from the railing and looked at Andrew. "What are you talking about? It's perfect."

Andrew pointed at a clump of alder bushes downstream. "See how the current flows through those trees over there? You'd go down in a second as soon as the dinghy hit them. It'd be full of holes."

"So we portage around the bushes," Matt said.

"Onto what? There's no solid ground anywhere around there. Besides, you wouldn't have a chance. The water's moving so fast the dinghy would be impaled on those trees before you knew what hit you."

"Andrew's right, Matt," Chad said.

Matt frowned. "Aw, all you guys ever do is look for problems. I think we should just throw the boat in the water tomorrow and see what happens. Even if we sink, we'll be wearing life jackets. Besides, it's Milligan Creek. How deep could it be?"

"Over your head in some places I'd say," Andrew replied. "Plus, that water is freezing. You'd be lucky to last a few minutes."

Andrew, who planned to be a lifeguard at the local pool when he got older, knew all about survival times in cold water from swimming lessons.

He looked up at the gray sky. "And if the weather turns cold, it'll only make things worse."

Dean pointed at the water. "Look, an iceberg!"

As the boys turned to look, a huge, triangle-shaped piece of ice surfaced about ten feet from the bridge. It sank again as it passed beneath them.

Dean shivered. "Brrrr. There's no way you're getting me into that dinghy tomorrow."

"Don't worry about it. I guess none of us are going," Matt said, kicking a rock in disappointment. It skittered across the bridge and then disappeared into the rushing water.

"Good," Dean said. "It was a dumb idea anyway."

"I wouldn't say that," Andrew replied.

Matt's ears perked up. "What do you mean? I thought you said we couldn't do it."

"Not in a dinghy we can't." A hint of a smile crossed Andrew's face.

"Keep talking," Matt said, turning to grin at Chad.

"No, forget it. We can't—"

"Let him finish, Dean," Chad said. "You don't have to go if you don't want to."

"A dinghy won't work, because it's too soft," Andrew said. "We need something that can take a bit more punishment."

"Then we'll build a raft!" Matt said.

"Well, we could. But I was thinking about something even more seaworthy: canoes. My Uncle George has two old aluminum canoes out behind his shed that he hasn't used for ages. I bet he'd lend them to us if I asked him."

"Excellent, let's go call him right now." Matt was already on the way to his bike. "We can phone from Dean's house."

"Oh no you can't. My mom won't let you," Dean said.

"Sure she will." Matt hopped onto his bike. "Besides, she's not even home from work yet."

"No, but she specifically said she didn't want our phone used for any more of your crazy schemes."

Matt smiled. "Relax, Dean. It's not *my* plan; it's Andrew's. He'll make sure everything works out. Isn't that right, Andy?"

"We don't have to use Dean's phone, Matt," Chad said. "We can wait 'til we get home."

Dean shook his head and sighed. "Don't worry about it, Chad. You can use the phone. But only if Andrew makes the call."

"Righto, Sir Worrywart," Matt said.

"Hey, give him a break," Chad replied, trying hard not to smile.

Dean hung his head. "I just don't want to see you all get killed."

Chad laid a hand on his worried friend's shoulder. "It'll be all right, Dean. Andy'll make sure we do this safely. Right?"

"Of course," Andrew replied.

Dean stared down at the rushing water and shivered. "I sure hope so."

Andrew's Uncle George said the boys were free to use his canoes, but only if their parents agreed to the venture. When Andrew phoned home to get permission from his parents, they told him they were invited to a barbecue at the Taylors' that night, so they could talk about it when they were all together. Andrew passed the news on to the rest of the guys.

"Excellent!" Matt said. "Hey, Dean, why don't you and your parents come, too?"

"I don't know . . .." Dean toed the floor and then looked up hopefully. "Will Joyce be there?"

Matt rolled his eyes. Dean had been in love with Matt and Chad's older sister, Joyce, since third grade.

"Of course she'll be there. But don't let her distract you. This is serious business."

"Yeah," Chad said. He punched Dean playfully in the shoulder.

Dean was unfazed. He picked up the phone. "Right. I'll just phone my mom at work and let her know." He tried to look nonchalant, but he couldn't restrain a huge grin from breaking out on his face.

Matt shook his head and laughed. "Make it quick, lover boy."

The other boys chuckled.

That night after a delicious supper of ham steaks, potatoes baked in foil, creamed corn, and strawberry pie, the three families held a conference around the Taylors' backyard fire pit. Feeling content after the big meal, they sat in lawn chairs clutching steaming mugs of hot chocolate that warmed their hands against the cool evening air.

Joyce, who was not overly fond of Dean's attention, had tried to avoid him all evening. But somehow he had still managed to nab a lawn chair right next to hers. She tried to sit as far away from him as possible without actually getting out of her chair. Dean, who was oblivious to her disinterest, sat with a grin on his face as he basked in the nearness of her presence.

"Well, I guess we've put you boys off long enough," Mr. Taylor said as he got up to throw more wood onto the fire. The other adults chuckled. They knew the boys had been practically bursting to talk about their plans from the moment everyone got together. Even Andrew, who rarely displayed much emotion, could scarcely contain his excitement.

Matt rose to his feet. "It's about time. Now, for those of you who don't know already, the reason we're gathered here tonight is to—"

"Eat some more of your sister's delicious strawberry pie?" Dean smiled dreamily at Joyce.

She rolled her eyes and scooted her chair even farther away. "Keep talking, Matt," Joyce said. "Keep talking!"

Dean slid his chair a little closer to hers.

She scooted away again. "And hurry!"

Matt glared at Dean before continuing. "As I was saying, we—being Chad, Andrew, Dean, and myself—would like to propose an adventure of the most amazing, most spectacular kind."

"What is it this time, Matthew? A voyage to the bottom of the lake in your homemade submarine?" Mrs. Loewen asked.

"No, he wants to make a flight in his pedal-powered glider," Mrs. Muller said. "From the top of the barn roof, no less." The parents laughed. The mention of those inventions hearkened back to two of the boys' earlier exploits, both of which turned out to be unqualified disasters. Thankfully, no one was hurt in either one.

"Yes, yes, all of your suggestions are quite amusing," Matt said. "And I know we've experienced many failures in the past. But this time I'm thinking much simpler than that. In fact, the adventure we are proposing is none other than a whitewater canoe trip—down Milligan Creek!"

The group was silent. A knot popped in the fire and sent sparks flying. Finally, Mr. Taylor spoke. "That's quite the idea, Matt. When would you want to leave?"

"Tomorrow morning."

Mr. Taylor's eyebrows shot up. "Tomorrow? You need time to prepare for a trip like that. Do you even know where you can get a canoe at such short notice?"

"Two canoes, actually," Matt said, "from Andrew's Uncle George."

Mr. Taylor glanced at Mr. Loewen, who nodded.

"Besides, we have to go tomorrow or the next day at the latest. Otherwise the water will have gone down too far," Andrew said. "The runoff only lasts a few days."

"I understand, Andrew," Mr. Taylor said, "but have any of you guys ever canoed before?"

"I learned how to do it last summer at camp," Andrew said. "I know all the strokes. We even went on an overnight trip to an island. I can teach these guys the basics in a jiffy. It'll all be very safe, Mr. Taylor. I've got our route all planned out."

Matt crossed his arms and smiled smugly. "See, Dad? We've got it all worked out."

"Yes, but canoeing in moving water is a lot different than paddling across a lake," Mr. Loewen pointed out.

"I've never canoed before," Dean said. "But that's okay, because I'm just going to stay on shore and watch." He turned to Joyce. "Maybe you can watch with me."

"No way," she said, shaking her head violently. "I'd rather—"

"That's okay, Joyce, I need you at home here tomorrow, anyway," Mrs. Taylor said.

Joyce gave her mother a thankful smile.

"If Dean isn't going in the canoe, who's going to be the fourth person?" Mrs. Taylor asked. "We can't have one of you boys in a canoe all by yourself."

The boys were quiet as they considered her question. The other three boys had been so excited about the trip that it hadn't even occurred to them that Dean might actually back out.

"How about if three of you go in one canoe?" Mrs. Loewen suggested.

Andrew shook his head. "Too tippy."

Matt looked at Mr. Taylor. "Hey, Dad, why don't you come? You always tell me how we should do more things together."

"I'm sorry, Matt, but I've got to fly a client up to Yorkton tomorrow." In addition to running his farm, Mr. Taylor owned a four-passenger plane that he took the boys up in from time to time when one of their shenanigans required it.

Matt turned to Mr. Muller. "How about you?"

"No can do, Matt. I'm booked solid all day tomorrow." Mr. Muller was an electrician. He also lent his expertise to help the boys in their various escapades.

His eyes pleading in desperation, Matt turned to Mrs. Taylor. "Mom?"

She shook her head, as did Mrs. Muller and Mrs. Loewen.

"There's no way I'm getting involved in one of your hare-brained schemes, Matt Taylor!" Mrs. Muller said. The other parents laughed.

"I'd love to do it, boys," Mr. Loewen said, "but someone has to drop you off and pick you up at the end, and I guess that's me."

Matt looked at Dean. So did Andrew and Chad. Dean shifted uneasily as their eyes burned into him.

"I told you I'm not going."

"But Dean, if you don't go, the entire trip will be off," Matt said.

"Would you feel better if you went in my canoe?" Andrew asked.

"No, I said forget it, I'm not going."

"I'll go then," Joyce said. "Is that okay, Mom?"

Dean gaped at her. "I thought you were busy."

"That's okay, I can do without her for tomorrow, I guess," Mrs. Taylor said, trying to suppress a smile.

Dean frowned. "Wait a minute. On second thought, maybe I do want to go."

"I don't know, Dean. It's going to be pretty scary out there," Chad said. "Tons of rapids and icebergs. You probably should let Joyce take your place." He winked at Matt and Andrew.

"No, no I think I should go." Dean turned to Joyce. "If you don't mind, that is. It's just that I would hate to see you get hurt."

Joyce tried to keep a straight face. "Why, thank you, Dean. You're so kind—and brave."

Dean beamed.

"Okay, it's settled then. We leave tomorrow morning at nine." Matt stood up to warm his hands over the fire and then stopped. "Oh, I mean if that's okay with you, Mr. Loewen."

Mr. Loewen nodded, his eyes on the fire. "I think I'll have had enough beauty sleep by then. What route are you planning to take, Andrew?"

Andrew stood up and cleared his throat. "Well, in the interest of safety, I think the best route is straight through town. That way we're never far from help, and you'll be able to keep your eye on us the entire way. We can put in at the highway bridge on the south side of town and get out by the graveyard bridge."

Mr. Loewen nodded. "Sounds good to me." He looked at Mr. Taylor and Mr. Muller. They nodded. "Okay then, well, we better all turn in early tonight." He drained his hot chocolate and then stood up. The other adults followed suit.

"Say a special prayer for Dean tonight, too" Matt said as he clapped Dean on the shoulder. "He looks like he needs it."

Everyone laughed. Dean tried to smile, but there was no way he could erase the worried expression from his face.

Despite her annoyance with him, Joyce laid a comforting hand on his shoulder. "Don't worry, Dean, you'll be fine."

At the sound of her voice—not to mention the touch of her hand—Dean's face brightened. It was all Joyce could do not to roll her eyes.

After everyone said their goodbyes, Matt, Chad, and Joyce helped their parents bring the food and dishes back into the house. As Matt passed Joyce, he smiled.

"Thanks, Joyce. We owe you one."

She grinned back. "I won't forget it. And be careful tomorrow."

"We will, right, Chad?" He turned to his brother, who had come up behind them.

"Of course, aren't we always?" Chad broke out into a huge grin as he shoved a leftover piece of ham into his mouth.

"Don't get me started," Joyce replied.

They all laughed as they went inside.

3

BON VOYAGE!

The following morning, the Taylor household bustled with activity as everyone helped prepare for the trip. Mrs. Taylor was making a lunch for the boys who, despite their excitement, had slept in and were wolfing down their breakfast so they would be ready when Andrew and his dad came to pick them up. Mr. Taylor had already left on his flight.

"Thanks for making our lunches, Mom," Chad said, as he wiped his mouth and then put his bowl and cup in the dishwasher.

Mrs. Taylor smiled. "You're welcome. But remember, not many kids have such a wonderful mother to depend on."

"I know. You're the best, Mom." Matt said. He gave her a kiss.

Just then the phone rang.

"I'll get it." Matt picked up the receiver. "Hello?" He listened and then smiled. "Oh, hello, Dean. So you're not feeling too good, hey?"

He grinned at Chad and shook his head. Chad slapped himself in the forehead and chuckled. Mrs. Taylor smiled as she sliced the boys' sandwiches.

"So, you don't think you can do the trip, huh?"

Just then Joyce wandered into the kitchen in her pajamas and opened the fridge, still bleary-eyed with sleep. "Who's on the phone?"

Matt winked at Chad. "Uh-huh, you had a tough night, I see. Well, I'll tell you what, so did Joyce, and you just woke her up with your phone call." He listened. "Yep, that's right. No, she doesn't look angry right now."

Joyce rolled her eyes. "Dean." She grabbed the jug of orange juice and shut the fridge door.

"But I think she might get angry when I tell her that she has to leave in five minutes to go canoeing with us."

Joyce stopped short. "What? Let me talk to him." She grabbed for the phone, but Matt waved her away.

"Oh, so you think you might be able to make it after all? Good. Yep, we're leaving right away, as soon as Andy gets here. Okay, see you then." Matt hung up.

"He's coming?" Chad asked.

"He's coming." Matt turned to his sister. "Thanks to Joyce and her incredible powers of persuasion."

"You can leave me out of your little escapades from now on, please." Joyce said as she headed back to her bedroom with a glass of juice. "By the way, have fun on your little trip—and don't do anything stupid."

Just then, a vehicle drove onto the yard. Mrs. Taylor looked out the window. "Andrew and Mr. Loewen are here. Quick, grab your lunches."

She followed Matt and Chad to the door and watched as they put on their jackets and boots. "Have you got everything?"

"Yeah. Dad put our stuff out last night. We just need to throw it in the truck," Matt said.

"Okay, we'll see you when you get back. Have fun, but most of all, be careful. And don't be too hard on Dean."

She kissed them both.

"All right, Mom. We will be—and we won't be," Matt said.

"Bye, Mom!" Chad waved as he followed Matt out the door.

Outside, Mr. Loewen's pick-up rumbled in the driveway, sending plumes of blue exhaust swirling into the chilly air. The rising sun glistened off the frosty undersides of the two aluminum canoes that were strapped in the truck box. They were scratched and dented, but to Matt and Chad, they couldn't have looked more perfect.

"Yikes, it's chilly out there," Matt said as he bounded into the truck. He reached over and cranked up the heater. "Ah, that's better." He warmed his hands over the vent.

"Hey, turn that off, it's boiling in here," Andrew said as he turned the heater off.

"Okay boys, let's not argue about it. We can keep it on low." Mr. Loewen turned the heater back on. "Now, have you got all your gear?"

Matt pointed out the window. "Yeah, if you'll drive us over to the shop we'll throw it in."

Andrew stared at him. "It's only twenty-five feet away. Can't you walk?"

"Are you kidding?" Matt rubbed his hands together over the vent.

Mr. Loewen chuckled. "Don't worry, fearless adventurers, it'll warm up soon enough." He slid the truck into reverse.

At the shop, Matt and Chad leapt out of the truck and grabbed their life jackets off the workbench. Chad looked around. "That's funny. I thought Dad said there was a bunch of stuff we were supposed to take."

"Guess he changed his mind," Matt said. "Come on." He held the door open for Chad. Chad took one last look around and then shrugged and went out.

Once they got to town, Mr. Loewen and the boys pulled up to Dean's house and honked. A moment later, Dean stumbled out the front door carrying a mountain of gear. In addition to a bulging backpack, his arms were full of extra clothes, a life jacket, his lunch box, and a paddle. A camera and a pair of binoculars were slung around his neck. Mrs. Muller stopped him on the front step and gave him a goodbye kiss. He tried to rub it off his cheek and ended up dropping his paddle. Mrs. Muller picked it up and handed it to him. She waved and then went back inside.

Dean started down the driveway, but he kept dropping things as he walked. When he stopped to pick them up, more things fell until nearly everything was on the ground, including his lunch box, which had popped open and sent his apple rolling down the driveway.

Mr. Loewen laughed. "One of you guys had better help him, or he'll never make it to the truck, never mind the creek."

Chad opened the door and jumped out. Matt was right behind him.

"Dean, you didn't have to bring everything you owned," Matt said. "We're only going to be gone for a couple of hours."

"Tell that to my mom," Dean replied. "She wanted me to take even more stuff, but I told her the boat would sink if I brought it all."

"It's not a boat, it's a canoe," Andrew said, as he came up behind Matt and Chad.

"Whatever." Dean picked up his gear.

Matt bent down to help him. Then he stood up in surprise, holding a copy of *Sports Illustrated*. "You brought a magazine?"

Dean shrugged. "In case I get bored."

Matt stared at him. "On a whitewater canoe trip? I doubt it. Leave it here." He tossed it aside.

"You can leave those binoculars at home, too, if you want," Andrew said. "I've already got a pair."

"You won't need that paddle either," Matt added.

"What are you talking about? Of course he needs a paddle," Andrew said.

Matt looked at him. "Well, we didn't bring any."

"Why not?"

"I thought they came with the canoes."

"Oh, shoot," Andrew said. "I forgot to phone you. Turns out my uncle only had one paddle. Do you have any more, Dean?"

"Yeah, we've got another one. I'll go get it." He dropped his gear and went back inside.

"That's three. We still need one more. Do you guys have any at home?" Andrew asked.

"I think so," Matt said.

"Well, maybe my dad can go and pick it up while I run you all through a little canoeing refresher course," Andrew replied.

Matt frowned. "Refresher course?"

"Yes, to make sure everyone remembers their strokes. You're going to need that stuff out there today."

"That sounds like a good idea, Andrew," Chad said as he gathered up the rest of Dean's gear.

"I guess so," Matt replied. "But I think you're taking this whole trip way too seriously."

"We'll see about that," Andrew said.

Just then, Dean came out the front door with the second canoe paddle. While inside, his mom had burdened him with another pile of gear, which he was struggling to balance in his arms as he kicked the door shut. He just managed to get the door closed when he slipped on the first step, which was icy from the previous night's frost, and tumbled to the ground.

Matt tried not to laugh. "Dean, are you okay?"

Chad, who was also trying not to laugh, ran up and helped Dean to his feet.

"I knew this trip was a stupid idea," Dean grumbled as he stomped off toward the truck.

Matt and Andrew exchanged amused glances. Chad scowled at them as he hefted an armload of gear. "Come on, you guys, quit fooling around and help out. You should be thankful Dean is even coming."

Matt blushed. "You're right, Chad. I'm sorry." He picked up Dean's life jacket and then ran off to help him and Chad load the truck.

A few minutes later, Mr. Loewen dropped the boys and the canoes beside the bridge south of town and then headed back to the Taylors' farm for the extra paddle.

After they checked out the creek, which was running even higher than the day before, Andrew led the boys through a brief review of the basic canoe strokes.

"Okay, if you'll all pay attention we can get through this quickly," Andrew said, using an official tone of voice. "Chad, can you come up here and demonstrate the basic forward stroke?"

Chad stepped up beside Andrew and started paddling an imaginary canoe.

"Excellent, see how he brings the paddle straight back and then gently curves it up out of the water? Do it exactly like that. Dean, let's see yours."

Dean knit his brow in concentration and pretended to paddle.

"That's good, Dean, but you need to grip your paddle on top. Here, like this." Andrew demonstrated by putting his palm on the top of the paddle. Dean followed his example. "Good, good, just like that."

Andrew turned to Matt. "Now, how about—"

He stopped short. Matt wasn't there. Andrew looked around until he spotted him stepping gingerly across the ice-encrusted snowbank that ran along the shoreline.

"Matt, get over here," Chad said.

Matt held a finger to his lips. "Shhh . . . You might cause the snowbank to crack." He took another step.

Andrew stepped toward him. "Careful, Matt. Sometimes the water flows under the snow and makes an overhang that weakens the—"

"Aaaaagh!" Matt yelled as half of the snowbank sank into the water. He tried to scramble back onto solid ground, but his movement only made things worse. In less than a second, he was chest deep in the water. He gasped at the sudden rush of cold. "Help!" he croaked.

Andrew leaped into action immediately. "Chad, grab my paddle!"

He grabbed onto a tree branch and held out his paddle for Chad. Chad grabbed it and, in turn, held out his paddle for Matt, who had slipped a few feet downstream and was holding onto a bush to prevent himself from being pulled away by the current. Matt got hold of Chad's paddle and pulled himself to shore, nearly pulling Chad into the creek in the process. Chad and Andrew grabbed his jacket and hauled him up onto the grassy bank.

"Oh man, that water's c-c-cold," Matt said. He rubbed his hands together vigorously, his teeth chattering.

Just then the boys heard the roar of Mr. Loewen's truck returning.

"Right on time," Andrew said. "Get those clothes off. I have some extra ones in the truck. You can get in there and warm up, too."

As Andrew led Matt off to the vehicle, Chad spotted Dean. He was rooted in place, his paddle still frozen in the finishing position of the stroke Andrew had been showing him just before Matt fell into the water.

Chad laid a hand on Dean's shoulder. "He'll be all right, Dean."

Dean bit his lip and watched the creek swirl and boil with the current.

"Dean," Chad said. "Are you okay?"

Dean turned away from the water and looked at Chad. "Yeah, I'm all right. I'm just really afraid of the water, especially cold water."

"Well, why don't you canoe with me? I'll make sure that the only thing that gets wet is your paddle. Sound like a plan?"

Dean nodded. "Thanks, Chad."

They both looked back as the truck door opened, and Matt jumped out wearing Andrew's extra clothes.

"Well, I guess that won't be the last time someone gets wet today, hey Dean?" He clapped him on the shoulder. Dean's face went rigid.

"Matt." Chad motioned for his brother to be quiet.

Matt nodded his understanding. "Sorry." He rubbed his hands together. "Well, I guess it's time we got these canoes in the water."

All four boys went back to the truck to help Mr. Loewen unload them.

"Looks like you cleared away a nice launching spot for us, Matt." Mr. Loewen nodded at the spot where the snowbank had fallen away.

"Anything to help," Matt said.

Once the boys had their life jackets on and everything else packed into the canoes, they carried them down to the water.

"Okay, who's going with who?" Mr. Loewen asked.

"Dean is with me," Chad said.

"Excellent," Matt replied. "That means I'm with Andrew. We'll take the lead."

"Okay. I'll watch you for a bit to make sure you're all right," Mr. Loewen said. "But then I'm going downtown to grab a few things before I meet you at the other end." Mr. Loewen looked at his watch. "That should be at around eleven thirty. If you get there before I do, you can just beach the canoes and walk down to Dean's place and wait for me. Remember: Don't go any farther than the graveyard bridge. If you do, you'll probably wind up stranded in the middle of somebody's field and have to walk home, carrying the canoes with you. Got it?"

"Got it," the boys replied in unison.

"Good. Now why don't you get in and I'll push you off. Matt and Andrew, you go first."

"Whoo-hoo!" Matt leapt into the front of his canoe. Andrew climbed in after him, and then Mr. Loewen pushed them into the creek. They paddled out of the current and waited for Chad and Dean to get in.

Just then, they heard a honk. They looked up and saw the Taylors' truck pull up beside Mr. Loewen's. Mr. and Mrs. Taylor and Joyce got out.

"Hey look, it's Mom and Dad!" Matt said. "And Joyce," he added, in Dean's general direction.

"Looks like we made it for the big send off," Mr. Taylor said. "Hi, Fred."

The two men shook hands as Mrs. Taylor snapped a picture of the boys.

"Yes, you made it. But you missed Matt's big splash," Mr. Loewen replied.

"Someone got wet already? That's not a good sign," Mr. Taylor said.

Dean's eyes went wide.

"Okay, boys, hang on." Mr. Loewen pushed the canoe into the water. Dean, who was sitting in the front, gripped the sides of the canoe until his knuckles were white.

"Bon voyage!" Mrs. Taylor smiled and waved to the boys. "We'll see you at the first bridge!"

"See you, Mom!" Chad waved his paddle and then faced forward. "Let's head over to Matt and Andrew," he said to Dean. When there was no response, he prodded Dean in the back with his paddle. "Dean, you can let go of the sides now."

Dean looked down at his hands, which still gripped the sides of the canoe. "Oh, right. Okay." He picked up his paddle.

"And we're off!" Matt said as Chad and Dean came up alongside them. He raised his paddle into the air. "To the graveyard—or bust!"

"Graveyard?" Dean asked.

The other boys couldn't help but laugh as Dean's face went white.

4

It's a UFO!

Matt dug his paddle deep into the water and swung the bow of his canoe into the current. It swept the vessel sideways and pulled it into the stream.

Andrew kept his paddle in the water and used it as a rudder as the canoe pulled away from shore. "I should be able to handle the steering from back here, Matt," he said. "I'll let you know if I need any help."

"Sounds good," Matt replied. "I'll just keep an eye out for rocks—and icebergs." He leaned forward until he was lying on the bow of the canoe, his face peering down at the water. "Wow, I can't see a thing. It sure must be deep here."

Andrew stuck his paddle into the water and tried to reach bottom. When his hand was completely submerged, he pulled it back out and held up the dripping paddle. "At least five feet I'd guess, maybe more."

"Probably way more." Matt slid back into his seat. The canoe wobbled from side to side as he settled himself.

"Easy." Andrew put his hands on the gunnels and steadied the canoe. "Unlike you, I don't plan on going for a swim today."

"It wasn't so bad," Matt said, struggling to prevent

his teeth from chattering. "On second thought, maybe it was."

Andrew laughed.

Matt turned back to see where Chad and Dean were. The two boys had just pulled into the current.

"Hold up, Andrew, let's wait for those slowpokes." Matt dragged his paddle in the water and then back paddled to slow them down.

"I thought you said you wanted to be in the lead," Andrew said.

"Yeah, but not this much of a lead. We're a team; we've got to stick together."

The boys pulled out of the current into some flooded bushes and waited until Dean and Chad caught up. Andrew and Matt each held onto a branch and reached out with their paddles so the other boys could grab hold and pull up alongside them.

"How's it going, Dean? Trying out those strokes I taught you?" Andrew asked.

"Yeah, sort of. This current basically moves us wherever it wants us to go."

Andrew nodded. "You can let Chad do the steering. I think this is actually going to be a lot easier than we thought. Just sit back and enjoy the ride."

Dean nodded. "I'll try."

"Hey guys, don't you think we're forgetting something?" Matt asked.

Chad looked at him. "What's that?"

Matt thumped the side of his canoe. "Names. We didn't name our boats."

"Canoes," Andrew said.

"Whatever."

"But they're not even ours," Dean objected.

"So what?" Matt said. "You can't have a boat—canoe—

without a name. It's bad luck."

"I know a good name for ours," Chad said.

Dean turned around to face him, struggling to see him over top of his oversized life jacket. "What's that?"

"Unsinkable."

Dean smiled. "I like it!"

"I thought you would." Chad reached forward, and they did an awkward high five in their life jackets.

Matt turned to Andrew. "Okay, what's the name of our canoe going to be?"

Andrew furrowed his brow as he thought about it. "I don't know . . ."

"I got it," Matt said. "UFO."

Dean turned to look at his friend. "Why would you pick a name like that?"

"Because when people see us going down the creek today, the first thing they're going to do is turn to each other and say, 'What the heck is that unidentified floating object? Get it? U-F-O."

Chad smiled. "I like it."

"Yeah, sure beats our name," Dean agreed. "No offense, Chad."

"Okay, we've got our names, now let's get out of here. You guys don't fall so far behind this time though," Matt said as he pushed the other boys back into the current. "Got it?"

"Got it," Chad said. "Catch us if you can! Let's go Dean!"

With that, Dean and Chad dug their paddles into the roiling black water and pulled away from Andrew and Matt.

"Come on, Andy, they're getting away!" Matt cried.

The boys paddled furiously, but the current kept pushing them back toward the bank.

"What's going on?" Matt asked, looking around in confusion.

"Seems like we're caught in an eddy," Andrew replied. "Just keep paddling. We'll catch them." Andrew eyed the water, searching for the fastest section of water.

With a few more strokes, Matt and Andrew heaved themselves out of the backwater and into the main flow. Soon they caught up to Chad and Dean, who were drifting along as they took in the sights. The boys watched as the creek wound its way through a stand of bushes laced with brown, dead grass, the branches wavering in the current. Huge banks of snow still clung to much of the shoreline, although a lot of it had already been washed away by the runoff. Red-winged blackbirds and sparrows flitted back and forth between the trees as the boys passed, as if excited at the prospect of the warm spring days to come.

As they rounded the final curve before the old cement highway bridge, the boys saw their parents watching and waving. At that moment, the sun came out from behind a patch of cloud, as if on cue.

"Okay, try and make it look like you know what you're doing," Matt whispered. "We don't want them having second thoughts and deciding we should get out at the bridge."

"Right." Chad looked ahead at Dean. "Grip the top of the paddle, Dean, not the side. And remember: Joyce is watching." He winked at Matt.

Dean's brow furrowed with concentration as he glanced up at the bridge. "The top? Right. Like this?"

"Good," Andrew said.

Dean tried to pull his life jacket down from around his ears, but it kept riding up. "Man, I wish I could just take this thing off. It makes me look like a dork."

"Better a floating dork than a dead dork," Matt said.

"Funny." Dean plastered a smile on his face as they

drew closer to the bridge, trying to look every bit the intrepid adventurer.

"How's it going boys?" Mr. Loewen called out. "You all manage to stay dry so far?"

"It's going great, Mr. Loewen," Matt said. "This is gonna be awesome!"

"Smile!" Joyce said as she held up her mother's camera. "This may be the last picture we ever get of you—alive!"

Dean blanched as Joyce snapped the shutter. She peeked around from behind the camera.

"I said smile, Dean, not frown!"

Everyone laughed as the canoes approached the bridge.

"Last chance to get out," Mr. Taylor said.

"Not on your life!" Matt replied, his voice echoing as they sailed under the bridge.

It took a second for the boys' eyesight to adjust to the darkness. But a flurry of flapping wings quickly brought their vision back into focus.

"Bats!" Dean cried, ducking forward in the canoe.

"Not bats, birds," Chad said as he also ducked to avoid them.

"Pigeons," Andrew clarified. "They must be nesting under here. Look!" He pointed up to the cement rafters where two gray-and-white pigeons sat next to each other on nests made of twigs.

"Check out those swallow nests over there," Matt said. "This is like some kind of bird sanctuary."

"Oh yeah? Then who wrote all that graffiti?" Chad said. The boys looked at the underside of the bridge and read a number of words that cannot be printed here.

"Man, the bigger kids must hang out under here when the water's lower. I never even knew this place existed," Matt said. "We'll have to check it out this summer."

"Suit yourself, Matt," Dean said. "You'll probably get beat up."

Matt shrugged as the bows of their canoes nosed out into the sunshine. "Maybe you're right."

As the boys pulled away from the bridge, they turned back and waved their paddles.

"See ya later!" Matt called.

"Bon voyage!" Mrs. Taylor said. Joyce snapped another picture, and then she joined the group as they walked back to their vehicles.

Once they were out of sight of the bridge, the boys settled back into their canoes as the creek meandered through a meadow of tall, thick slough grass, dotted here and there with clumps of willow bushes.

"We're on our own," Chad said.

Matt nodded. "Finally."

Dean looked back. "I sure hope Joyce is waiting for us at the other end. I can't wait to tell her all about the trip."

"Just keep focused, Romeo," Matt said. "You've got to have the adventure before you can tell her about it."

"Right." Dean faced forwards again. "You know, this isn't so bad. I really think I'm going to like this trip."

"Yes, the current is pretty slow here," Andrew said.

"Hopefully it speeds up later on," Matt replied.

"Oh, I'm sure it will," Andrew said. "Just think about how fast it was moving under the graveyard bridge."

"Awesome, let's go!" Matt dug in his paddle.

The boys paddled through the meadow until they reached a spot where an old road, really nothing more than a two-lane track, dipped down into the tiny gully where the creek flowed and then up the other side. The lowest part of the road was completely submerged. Normally, it connected the street where the police station was located with a secondary highway that passed through town.

"What's that?" Dean asked as he pointed to a small, square cement building.

"A pump house," Andrew said. "It pumps water from the reservoir—where this creek starts—to the water tower." Andrew pointed to a tall, thin tower with a big ball on top. The name "Milligan Creek" was written across the ball in big black letters. It looked like a huge white lollipop.

"I always wondered what that thing was for," Dean said as he eyed the tower. "Wait a second, what is it for?"

"To create water pressure," Andrew said. "At the top of the tower is a huge water tank. The higher you go, the more pressure you create. That's what makes the water flow out of your taps."

"I never knew that. You're pretty smart," Dean said.

Andrew shrugged. "You'll learn all about it in grade seven science."

"I wonder if we could ever get inside that thing," Matt said eagerly.

"I don't know, maybe," Andrew said. "We should ask sometime. Do a class field trip."

"I heard about a town where they found a dead guy in their water tower," Chad said. "He'd been in there for six months or so."

"Gross!" Dean shuddered. "I sure hope they check ours regularly."

"He wasn't actually in the water," Chad said. "Just got stuck in the tower somewhere."

"It's still gross."

"Hey, check that out." Matt pointed ahead with his paddle to where the creek opened up into a large pool. It had flooded the backyards of several homes located along the creek, causing the current to disappear.

Chad leaned forward and peered at something silver that flashed between a row of trees up ahead. "Is that a fence? It looks like barbed wire."

"You may be right, Chad," Andrew said. "We'll have to go over to the right."

The boys paddled in that direction, cruised between the trees, and into the backyard.

"This is so cool," Matt said. He pointed up the bank with his paddle. "That's Mrs. Halverson's place. I used to play there when I was a little kid. Wow, totally flooded. The water's practically up to her doorstep."

"Look, there's someone's bridge," Dean said. "It must have floated away." He pointed over to some bushes where a small, homemade bridge had gotten lodged after breaking free from its moorings.

"Hey, that gives me an idea," Matt said. "Come on, Andrew, let's head for it."

The two boys paddled toward the bridge until they reached the far side of it. They turned the canoe around until the bow was pointed toward the bridge.

"Check this out!" Matt called to the other boys. Then he and Andrew paddled down the middle of the floating bridge.

"Too funny," Dean said as he snapped a picture. Then he looked at his watch. "C'mon, let's get going. I don't want Mr. Loewen to start worrying about what's taking us so long."

"Yeah, and I want to find some rapids!" Chad said.

"Not with me in here you don't!" Dean replied.

Chad grinned sheepishly. "Sorry."

As the boys paddled through the flooded backyards, they saw picnic tables, swing sets, and barbecue pits all submerged under at least three feet of water.

"I've never seen the creek so high!" Matt said.

"Warm weather over the past couple of days, it looks like all of the snow is melting at once," Andrew said.

The boys pulled out of the trees and headed toward

Marchuck Street, which ran parallel to the creek.

A few moments later, they heard a car honk. They looked up and saw several vehicles had slowed down to watch them. The boys waved with their paddles, and the people waved back. One rather large lady with long white braids got out of her car and started snapping pictures.

"Hey, that's Judy Yearwood," Dean said. "She's a reporter for the *Milligan Creek Review*. Wow, we're going to be in the paper!"

"Smile pretty, boys," Matt said.

"Yeah, I can read the headline now," Chad said. "UFO Sighted in Milligan Creek!"

"You got it!" Matt replied, grinning.

A few moments later, the creek turned away from the road and flowed back into the trees. The boys gave a final wave to their "fans" and then disappeared from sight.

Soon they were surrounded by low scrub bush dotted with occasional stands of poplar and birch.

Dean, who was enjoying himself so much he had practically forgotten about his fear of the water, looked forward and spotted something swimming up ahead of them. "Hey, what's that?" he asked. "Looks like an otter."

"There aren't any otters around here," Andrew replied. He peered ahead at the creature. "It's a beaver. Look, he's got a branch in his mouth. Must be bringing it home for lunch."

"Beavers eat branches?" Dean asked.

"Not branches, just the bark," Andrew said. "But he may not be planning to eat it. He may use it to build up his dam."

"He'll need a pretty big dam to stop all this water," Matt said.

Andrew scanned the shoreline. "His lodge must be around here somewhere. Just keep your eye out for it."

"There it is!"

The boys looked over to where Dean was pointing and saw a massive pile of mud and sticks nestled against the bank. "Wow, must be a ton of them living in there."

As the beaver drew near to its home, it glanced back at the boys, raised its tail, gave the water a slap, and then dove beneath the surface with a huge splash.

"Cool!" Dean exclaimed. "Did you see his tail?"

"Guess he's not a UFO buff," Chad said. The other boys laughed.

"Hey, what's that?" Matt asked. The boys looked ahead and saw a line of white water stretching across the creek.

"Rapids!" They all said in unison.

"I'll bet that's the beaver's dam," Andrew said. "It's totally flooded, and the water is pouring over it."

"Let's go for it!" Matt dug in his paddle and pulled the canoe forward.

A short way behind him, Dean sat in the bow of his canoe, his paddle poised motionless in the air. "I can't go over rapids, Chad."

"Sure you can. Look, just sit back and stay low in the canoe, and I'll handle everything."

Dean glanced warily at the rapids and then set his paddle into the canoe. He knelt down on the floor and grasped the gunnels while Chad pushed them forward.

"Don't worry," Chad said. "Just hang on."

"Okay, Chad. But remember: I'm trusting you."

Chad and Dean watched as Andrew and Matt drew close to the rapids. Andrew called out directions to Matt to make sure they hit the rapids dead on. Matt paddled furiously, his eyebrows knit together in concentration. Seconds later, they sailed right over them.

"Man, that was nothing," Matt said as he and Andrew turned the canoe around so they could watch Chad and

Dean go through. "Let's see how those guys do."

"Ready, Dean?" Chad asked.

Dean nodded slightly.

"Then let's go! Whoo-hoo!"

Chad paddled hard for a few more strokes and then raised his paddle as their canoe sailed over the flooded dam. Once they were through, they paddled over to the slack water, where Matt and Andrew were waiting.

"Pretty lame, hey?" Matt said.

Chad shrugged. "Better than nothing. I'm sure there'll be more."

"I hope so," Matt replied.

"That actually wasn't so bad," Dean said as he picked up his paddle.

"Oh yeah? Are you sure you didn't leave dents in the side of the canoe with your fingernails?" Matt said, laughing.

"Knock it off, Matt," Chad said, scowling at his younger brother.

"Sorry, Dean. I was just kidding around."

"Okay, let's keep moving," Andrew said. "We've still got a long way to go."

The creek continued to wind through town. Sometimes the boys sailed past people's houses, at other times they were back in the woods. The current was moving swiftly but not so fast the boys could not handle it. Soon even Dean was beginning to feel like an old pro.

"We should be turning back toward Marchuck Street soon," Andrew said. "We'll have to keep our eye out for the culverts. I'm not sure whether we'll be able to go through them or not."

"Culverts?" Dean asked.

"Of course we'll be able to get through them," Matt said. "Don't you remember walking through them during the summer when we were down here catching leeches?"

"Yes, but this water is really high, way higher than I expected."

Dean swallowed hard.

A few moments later, the boys rounded a final bend and pulled out of the woods. They were facing Marchuck Street directly and could just see the grain elevators of Milligan Creek poking above the trees to their right across the railway tracks. The culverts were dead ahead. True to Andrew's word, the five-foot high, corrugated aluminum tubes were almost completely engorged with water.

The boys hadn't noticed it, but over the last hundred yards, the creek had narrowed somewhat, causing the current to nearly double in speed. As they rounded the bend, they realized they were going way too fast to stop.

Matt stared in horror at the rushing water straight ahead of them. "Uhhh . . . Andrew?"

"I'm thinking, I'm thinking!" Andrew said. "Back paddle!"

The boys paddled backwards as hard as they could.

"I can't slow down!" Dean cried as his and Chad's canoe swept past.

"Keep trying!" Andrew grunted as he dug his paddle into the water.

"No, not that side, on the left!" Chad said.

Dean switched to the other side, nearly dropping his paddle in the process. "Forward or backward?"

"Forward!"

Try as they might, Chad and Dean could not turn their canoe one way or the other.

Chad paddled frantically as Dean sat frozen in the bow staring at the black water rushing through the left culvert, pulling them closer.

"Chad, does it look like you can make it through?" Andrew asked.

Chad peered forward. "I don't know!"

"No time!" Andrew said. "Just aim straight for it and duck. You too, Dean!"

Dean hesitated for a moment and then threw down his paddle and hit the deck. Chad kept steering right up until the last moment and then dove forwards onto the floor of the canoe. Matt and Andrew watched helplessly as the canoe disappeared into the culvert.

"They're in!" Matt cried.

"Yeah, but can they make it through?"

"Too late to worry about that," Matt said, their own canoe rushing straight toward the other culvert.

"Duck!"

5

CULVERTED!

At the last second, Matt and Andrew both lay back, and then their canoe was sucked into the silver metal tube. It was dark inside, but as they boys lay on their backs, they could just make out the bolts that held the culvert together mere inches above their heads.

"Cool!" Matt said. "If the water were even an inch higher, I don't think we would have made it."

Just then, the bow of their canoe started bumping against the ridges on the top of the culvert, where it dipped toward the middle of the road.

"Andrew!"

"Just think heavy thoughts!"

Matt grimaced. "I just hope the water's not any higher in the other culvert!"

"Me, too," Andrew replied.

The water was just low enough to allow the canoe to make it through. Despite his excitement, Matt could not help but feel relieved when they emerged on the other side and discovered Chad and Dean waiting for them.

"Congratulations, guys," Chad said. "You've just been 'culverted.' Cool, hey?"

"Awesome!" Matt said. "I want to do it again!"

"Forget it," Andrew said. "I'm not lugging this canoe up that bank."

"Yeah, I guess you're right," Matt replied as he stared longingly back at the road.

"How are you doing, Dean?" Andrew asked.

Dean squinted at him as the sun reflected off the water. "Not too bad. I was scared going in, but it was pretty cool once I knew we were going to make it."

"We got lucky," Andrew said. "The water was just low enough. I was worried about the edge of the culvert, too. It's sharp. It could probably take your head off."

"Now you tell us," Matt said.

Andrew shrugged. "I didn't want Dean to panic."

Matt smiled and tapped his head. "Always thinking, aren't you?"

Andrew grinned.

"I actually wouldn't mind doing that again," Dean admitted.

"That's the stuff!" Matt exclaimed. "Let's keep going! Maybe there'll be more culverts."

The boys pushed off and continued their journey downstream.

Soon the creek brought them past a small acreage on the edge of town. The red barn and dilapidated outbuildings looked inviting on the shore of the creek.

"I wish the creek was this high all year," Matt said. "This would make a great fishing spot."

Indeed, the water was beginning to spread out into more of a pond. The current slackened, and the boys found they had to paddle steadily to keep moving forward. The water was much shallower as well, only a couple of feet deep, and they had to keep an eye out for stumps, rocks, and other hazards. It wasn't long though before the boys heard the sound of rushing water once again.

"More rapids?" Matt asked hopefully.

"I don't think so," Chad said. "Look."

The boys looked ahead and saw that, instead of rapids, the sound was caused by the water as it flowed through several clumps of trees that nearly choked off the creek.

"Great, how are we going to get through that?" Dean asked.

"Looks like we'll have to portage," Andrew said.

"Poor what?" Dean asked.

"*Portage*. It's a French word that means 'to carry your boat from one body of water to another' or something like that."

"What? You want us to carry our canoes?" Dean looked down at the water. "I'm not getting my feet wet."

"Then you'd better make yourself comfortable, because you'll be sitting here until the runoff dies down," Andrew said.

"Yeah, come on, Dean, don't be such a baby," Matt said. "It's not even up to your knees. Your rubber boots will keep it out."

Dean sighed. "All right."

The boys let their canoes drift toward the trees until they spotted a gap large enough to squeeze through. Matt and Chad, who were just wearing sneakers, jumped out into the water. It was almost up to their knees.

"Whew, that's cold," Matt said as he grabbed the bow of his canoe and swung it toward the opening in the trees. Andrew was about to get out when Matt stopped him. "No sense us all getting wet if we don't have to."

"Now you tell me," Dean said, having just climbed out of his canoe. "And the water is so over my boots!" He tried to get back into the canoe and nearly fell into the water.

Chad laughed and shook his head. "You might as well just stay out now, Dean. Your feet are already wet."

Dean glared at him and then grabbed hold of his canoe. "In the canoe, out of the canoe, make up your mind!" He sighed. "Let's just get this over with. I'm just glad my mom talked me into bringing extra socks."

Chad chuckled to himself.

Within a few minutes, the boys were able to push their canoes through the trees and into a deeper section of water. By that point, however, the boys' pants were soaked up to their thighs.

"Okay, so how do we get back in?" Dean asked.

"Put one foot in first, and place it in the center of the canoe," Andrew said. "Then grab the gunnels—the sides of the canoe—and pull yourself in. And remember: keep low."

Dean did as he was told and managed to heave himself into the canoe. Chad and Matt followed suit, and soon the boys were off.

They made good time over the next stretch. The sun was high, and they were able to relax and enjoy the scenery as the creek meandered back and forth between the trees on a large, vacant piece of property. It was overgrown with grass and clumps of alder and willow trees. A few old, rusted-out cars were also partially submerged in the deluge. The boys heard vehicles going by on the highway off to their left. It led north out of town toward the local resort lake, which was about fifteen kilometers away.

"Boy, it seems like we've gone quite a ways, but we haven't actually traveled very far," Dean said as he looked back.

"Yeah, the creek is really twisting back and forth," Andrew said. "It's not a very efficient way of getting around."

"Whatever that means," Dean said.

"He means it's slow," Chad said.

"Speaking of slow, isn't it time we stopped for a rest, maybe had a bite to eat?" Dean suggested.

Andrew looked at his watch and grimaced. "I don't

know, Dean. We're already way behind schedule."

"I wouldn't worry too much about that," Matt said. "There's the perfect spot for a picnic."

He lifted up his paddle and pointed to a grassy knoll along the creek. "We don't have to stay long, just long enough to grab a bite to eat—and dry off." Matt's teeth chattered. "I'm still pretty chilly from being wet anyway."

Andrew nodded. "Okay, I guess a fifteen-minute stop won't hurt."

The boys steered their canoes over to the bank and nudged them into the shoreline. Frogs skittered away from their feet as they stepped out into the waving grass that had been flooded by the runoff. They hauled the canoes up out of the water so they would not be dragged away by the current. Chad helped Dean haul his huge pack out of the canoe and up the bank while Andrew and Matt grabbed their lunch bags and found a nice dry spot in the middle of a patch of dry, dead grass that had been matted down from the snow. Matt peeled off his sopping wet shoes and socks and laid them out on the grass to dry. Then he lay back and drank in the warm April sun.

"What a perfect day," he said.

Andrew nodded as he sat down beside him and opened his lunch bag. He unwrapped a sandwich, took a bite, and squinted out at the meadow. The creek sparkled as it wound in and around the clumps of trees. "I sure love this time of year, before the leaves come out."

"Not to mention the mosquitoes," Matt said, sitting up. He leaned over and dug a sandwich out of his lunch bag.

Andrew nodded, his mouth full. "No kidding."

Chad and Dean plunked down next to the other two boys.

"Great spot," Chad said.

Dean tugged at his rubber boots, which were suctioned onto his feet by the water inside.

"Need a hand?" Chad asked.

"No way, not after the last time."

Matt and Chad laughed. Dean gave his boot a huge tug, and it came off with a pop. He turned it upside down to empty the water out and then threw it down on the grass and started tugging on the other one. Andrew eyed Dean's white cotton gym socks, which had turned brown from the mud and water.

"Should have worn wool socks," Andrew said between bites of his sandwich.

"Huh?" Dean glanced at Andrew as he yanked on his other boot.

Andrew reached down and pulled up his pant leg, revealing a gray woolen work sock with white trim and a red line around the top. "Wool keeps you warm whether it's wet or dry. All you have to do is wring them out."

"Now you tell me," Dean said as he yanked off his second boot. After he emptied the water out of it, he peeled off his socks and wrung them out.

"Any chance your mom talked you into bringing two extra pairs of socks?" Matt asked.

"As a matter of fact, she did," Dean said. "Why?"

Matt shrugged. "Just thought I might be able to borrow them."

"What's the point? Your shoes are soaked. You'll only get them wet again."

"Maybe, but your boots are soaked, too. You'll just get them wet anyway."

"Maybe, maybe not," Dean said. He dug into his backpack and pulled out a towel. "I'm going to try and dry them out."

The boys watched as Dean jammed the towel down into his right boot to soak up the water.

Chad lay back on the grass and put one arm behind his head as he munched on an apple. "We should do this again someday when we're older. On a real river."

"Yeah," Matt said, raising himself up on one elbow. "With some real rapids, not just water flowing over a flooded beaver dam."

"Don't give up on this creek yet," Andrew said. "We've still got a ways to go. We could still run into something exciting."

"As long as it's not more culverts," Dean said. "Now that I think about it, once was enough for me."

After their brief rest, the boys resumed their trip downstream, weaving their way back and forth across the meadow. They rounded a bend in the stream and saw the highway ahead of them, where they would pass beneath another old cement bridge.

As they neared the bridge, Andrew got a concerned look on his face. "You know, guys, it just occurred to me that this creek passes under the railway tracks at some point."

"Another bridge?" Matt asked.

Andrew shook his head. "I don't think so. Look."

He pointed ahead to the tracks, which were just coming into view. The rail bed towered a good fifteen feet above the water line, and the boys saw that the water was rushing beneath the tracks through three large cement culverts. Unlike the previous set of culverts, which were round and made out of metal, these ones were triangular and made out of cement. The current actually slowed down before the culverts, forming a large pool. The rail bed was acting like a dam and the culverts like floodgates. They could not let the water through fast enough, so it was building up on the south side of the tracks.

"Should we get out and portage while we still have the chance?" Dean asked.

Andrew eyed the culverts carefully. "I don't know. Let's get a little closer. Keep close to the shoreline in case we need to get out."

The boys paddled cautiously ahead, never taking their eyes off the culverts. Behind them a few cars rumbled over the bridge and honked. The boys did not even turn around to wave.

"The right one looks jammed," Matt said. "It's full of logs and junk."

Andrew nodded. "Chad, can you see through the left one?"

Chad shook his head. "Nah."

"The middle one looks clear," Matt said. "I think we can make it."

"Okay, but be ready to pull out at the last minute if it doesn't look like we'll fit."

"Gotcha," Matt said, his paddle already in the water.

Dean and Chad watched anxiously as the other canoe was sucked toward the water rushing into the concrete tunnel.

"Looks good!" Matt called back over his shoulder as he leaned forward. "I can see daylight on the other side."

"Go for it!" Chad said. "We'll be right behind you!"

Matt and Andrew used their paddles to steer right up until the last second. Then they ducked as their canoe disappeared into the culvert. Chad and Dean heard them hooting and shouting as they went through, their voices echoing in the shadowy tunnel.

"I sure hope those aren't screams of pain and terror," Dean said.

Chad laughed. "I don't think so. Ready for round two?"

"I don't know," Dean said, eying the culvert warily. "I've got a bad feeling about this one."

"C'mon, Dean, this doesn't look nearly as scary as the last ones."

"I know, but—what's that?"

Chad looked around. "What's what?"

"Listen."

The boys grew quiet. At first, all they heard was the rumble of distant vehicles. Then they heard yelling. It was Matt and Andrew, only this time it didn't sound like they were having fun. They were afraid. One word in particular sent a chill down Dean's spine.

"Rapids!" he and Chad said in unison.

6

MAN OVERBOARD!

The moment Andrew and Matt emerged from the culvert, a powerful current seized their canoe and pulled them around a sharp turn to the left. The water rushed around the corner, plowing into the right bank on the way by. A large part of the bank had already been gouged out by the torrent. Worst of all, up ahead, overhanging the water at chest level was a huge, dead tree. Its gray branches jutted in all directions, some of them broken off into menacingly sharp points.

Matt and Andrew back-paddled frantically to avoid getting sucked into the tree.

"It's not working!" Matt said through clenched teeth as he jammed his paddle into the water.

"Keep trying!"

"I wish there was some way we could warn Chad and Dean!"

Just then, their canoe hit a submerged log and turned broadside.

"What was that?" Matt yelled.

"Duck!" was all Andrew had time to say before their canoe slammed into the tree, rode up one of the larger branches, and flipped over.

Matt was thrown against the tree. Half submerged in the rushing water, the only thing holding him up was his life jacket, which had been impaled on a sharp branch. He struggled to hold on as the current pressed him against the tree, threatening to suck him under.

"Andrew!" he yelled, his eyes scanning the raging water, but there was no sign of his friend. Just then, the branch that had impaled Matt's life jacket broke, and he sank deeper into the water, the current trying to force him under the water.

"Help!" he cried as he clung desperately to the tree.

At that moment, Chad and Dean, who had beached their canoe rather than risk going through the culvert, scrambled up the bank onto the railway tracks. They stopped short when they spotted Matt clinging to the tree.

"Oh no!" Dean cried. "Where's Andrew? And where's their canoe?"

"Come on!" Chad yelled, already running down the embankment toward Matt.

Matt had just managed to pull himself out of the water when he heard a splash. He looked up as Andrew popped to the surface a short way downstream, gasping like a dog that had been pushed into a swimming pool.

"Andrew, thank God. Are you okay?"

Andrew didn't say anything, just dog paddled toward shore, where he grabbed onto a tree branch so he could catch his breath, too weak and shaken even to pull himself out of the water.

Matt looked down and saw the canoe was hooked onto a branch just beneath the surface. He tried to reach it, but it was too deep. He looked around for something to help him dislodge it, and only then did he realize he was still holding onto his paddle! He turned back to Andrew, who had finally managed to haul himself out of the water.

"You okay?" Matt asked again.

Andrew nodded, but he still looked disoriented.

"Say something, Andy!"

"S-s-something," Andrew replied.

Matt smiled with relief. "So you are okay. Whew, that was some ride! You had me worried for a moment. I thought you were stuck on a branch under there."

Andrew nodded. "Me, too." His entire body shuddered from the cold.

Just then, Chad and Dean came crashing through the dense willow scrub along the side of the creek.

"Matt, are you okay?" Chad called as he ran up. "Where's Andrew?"

"Right there!" Matt pointed to where Andrew was huddled on the shore.

Dean paused and looked around. "Where's your canoe?"

Matt pointed at the water. "Down there."

"What happened to your life jacket?" Chad asked.

Matt fingered the hole where the branch had stabbed through. "I don't know how it missed me, but I'm sure glad it did."

Chad shook his head in amazement.

Dean eyed Andrew's huddled form with concern. "I thought you said the canoe wouldn't sink."

"It didn't sink," Matt said. "It's caught on a branch. Here, I'll see if I can reach it." He plunged his paddle beneath the icy water. He could just reach the canoe, but he could not budge it. "No good. I need to get deeper."

"Careful, Matt," Chad said, watching anxiously. "You don't want to get caught underwater on that tree. The current will hold you down."

Matt stepped down into the water, balancing himself on a submerged branch while holding onto another branch above his head. He braced himself against the current, which swirled around his legs, and then leaned over until his arm was submerged up to his shoulder. He was finally able to dislodge the canoe from the branch.

"It's free," he said as he climbed back out of the water.

Dean watched as the sunken canoe began to drift downstream. "It's getting away!" he said as he walked along the shoreline, keeping pace with it.

"Don't worry, I'll get it," Andrew said. He stepped back into the water, grabbed the canoe, and then heaved it toward shore. Chad and Dean rushed over to help.

Together, they flipped it over and dumped out the water. Then Andrew started to take off his wet clothes. Dean dug into his backpack and held out a towel.

"G-g-good thing your mom made sure you were prepared," Andrew said as he accepted the towel and dried himself off. "Thanks."

"No problem," Dean said. He dug into his pack and pulled out another towel. "You want one, too, Matt?"

"Sure."

When Matt unfurled the towel, it had a huge picture of Big Bird from Sesame Street on it and was customized with Dean's name. "Wow, didn't know you were such a fan," Matt quipped.

Dean reddened. "That was a long time ago, and it was my mom's idea, not mine."

"I don't care," Matt said. "Just as long as it's dry."

He grinned at Andrew as the boy struggled to take off his sopping wet jeans. "Bet you're glad you're wearing wool socks, hey Andy?"

"Funny," Andrew said, scowling.

Matt started to laugh, and pretty soon Andrew's face

cracked into a smile. Dean and Chad joined in as well, more out of relief than anything.

"So, what are we going to do now?" Chad asked.

"I say we pack it in, leave the canoes here, and walk the rest of the way to the graveyard bridge," Dean said.

Matt stared at him in astonishment. "Are you kidding?"

"Look at you guys," Dean replied. "Andrew nearly drowned, you're soaked, and you're already on your second set of clothes, Matt. Besides, our canoe is still on the other side of the tracks."

"That could be a problem, Matt," Andrew said. "I don't want either of us to get hypothermia." His body shook with another shiver.

"Hypo-what?"

"Never mind," Andrew said. "I'm just worried that we're going to get chilled sitting in these wet clothes."

Matt turned to Dean. "What else have you got in your pack?"

"Not much," Dean said, taking a step back. "Why?"

"Let's see," Matt said, striding forward.

Dean's face fell. "Aw come on, guys, haven't you had enough?"

"Open it up, Muller," Matt said.

Dean groaned. "Oh, all right. Here." He handed his pack to Matt. Matt knelt down on the grass and opened it. The first thing he pulled out was a huge bag of food.

"Awesome," Matt said. "Andrew and I lost what was left of our lunches when the canoe tipped over."

"I lost my favorite jacket, too," Andrew said, his eyes scanning the water. "It was lying on the bottom of the canoe. We'll have to keep an eye out for it."

"Right. Now, what else do we have here?" Matt dug out two more towels, two pairs of pants, a sweatshirt, and two

T-shirts. There was even an extra pair of running shoes on the bottom as well as a First-Aid kit and a survival pack.

Once he finished unpacking, Matt sat back in amazement. "Dean, who the heck is your mom, the captain of the search and rescue squad?"

Dean shrugged. "I don't know; she used to be a girl guide. You know, always be prepared."

"Mind if we borrow these clothes?" Matt asked.

Dean sighed. "Why not? We're almost done the trip anyway."

"I wouldn't say that," Matt replied.

A few minutes later, Andrew and Matt felt much better in dry clothes. Matt was even able to change out of his wet shoes and socks, but Andrew opted to keep his on. He was a true believer in the "wet or dry" wool sock theory.

"So, how do we look?" Matt asked.

"Like Dean," Chad said, laughing.

"Look, flood pants!" Dean said, pointing to Andrew's feet. Andrew was about six inches taller than Dean, so the borrowed sweat pants barely came down to his ankles.

"Perfect, just perfect," Chad said.

The other boys all laughed.

7

THE GRAVEYARD BRIDGE

Matt volunteered to go back with Chad and portage their canoe over the railway tracks. Thankfully, they were able to float it part of the way along the shoreline rather than carry it all the way. Once they got back to Andrew and Dean, the boys had everything packed up, and Andrew was standing next to his canoe with an old, gray wooden plank in his hand.

"What's that?" Matt asked.

"My new paddle," Andrew said as he patted the wood. "I found it in the bushes. It'll have to do until we find my real paddle. It's got to be somewhere ahead of us."

"Good idea," Matt said. "Now let's shove off!"

"Yeah, we don't want Joyce worrying about what might have happened to us," Dean said.

Matt grinned. "No, we definitely wouldn't want that!"

"There's the graveyard bridge," Chad called out about fifteen minutes later. Everyone looked up as they rounded a bend and saw the spot where the whole idea of canoeing down Milligan Creek had begun only a day earlier.

"The trip's over already? Bummer," Matt said.

"I would've thought you'd had enough already," Dean replied.

Matt shrugged. "We got a little wet, but even you have to admit it's been fun."

Dean thought about it for a moment and then nodded. "Yeah, I guess so."

"I know I won't forget it," Matt said. "And I don't think Andy will either." He turned back and grinned at Andrew.

"No bout a doubt it," Andrew said.

"Lame-o," Chad replied.

The boys paddled in silence, drinking in the final few moments of their voyage. They beached the canoes about twenty yards before the bridge. There were still only a few feet between the bottom of the bridge and the water, and the boys had no interest in seeing if their canoes could make it through.

Dean was the first one onto the shore. He knelt down and kissed it. "Dry land! Finally."

"Don't be so dramatic," Matt said. "You were walking around on land just a few minutes ago."

Once the canoes were stowed on shore, the boys sat down on the bridge and dangled their feet over the water as they waited for Mr. Loewen to arrive.

Andrew checked his watch. "He probably came once and left again after he didn't see us here. Thanks to our little accident, we're forty-five minutes past the time we said we'd arrive."

"Maybe he's checking upstream to make sure we didn't get stuck somewhere," Chad suggested.

"Or maybe downstream," Matt said and grinned.

"Nobody would think we'd be that stupid," Dean replied, looking downstream.

Matt followed his gaze with a longing look in his eye. "Stranger things have happened."

"Hey, what's that?" Chad asked. The other boys looked over to where he was pointing. The surface of the water was covered with a litter of foam, dead leaves, sticks, and other debris. Amongst it all was a familiar, blond-colored wooden object.

"Andrew's paddle!" Matt said.

Dean stood up. "It's getting away!"

Andrew scanned the shoreline and then ran over and picked up a long tree branch that had been washed ashore by the flood. "I'll try and snag it."

He dashed back to the bridge and then hung over the railing as far as he could and held out the branch. He just managed to hook the handle, but then he lost it again. The paddle slipped through and sailed on under the bridge.

"Lost it!" Dean said.

"Not yet!"

Andrew ran to the other side of the bridge. He reached out again with the branch, but it was too late. He and the other boys watched as the paddle disappeared downstream.

"My uncle's going to kill me."

"Sorry, Andy," Dean said as he put a hand on Andrew's shoulder.

A moment later, a sudden cry got their attention.

"Whoo-hoo!"

They turned around and saw Chad and Matt in their canoe, headed straight for the bridge.

"Don't worry, madam! We'll get your paddle for you!" Matt cried, a huge grin stretched across his face as he held his paddle in the air.

Dean's mouth fell open. "You'll never make it beneath the bridge!"

"Only one way to find out!" Matt said. "One, two, three—hit the deck!"

Matt leaned all the way back as if he was doing the limbo. Chad dove forward onto the bottom of the canoe.

Andrew and Dean ran over to the other side of the bridge just as Matt and Chad emerged unscathed.

"We did it!" Matt exclaimed. He turned back to face Andrew and Dean, who stood there, slack-jawed. "Be back in a jiff!"

"Oh yeah? How are you going to do that?" Andrew asked.

"We'll just put ashore somewhere. Don't worry about it," Matt said as he and Chad disappeared around the bend.

"Great," Dean said. "Just great. Now we're all in big trouble."

Andrew looked over at Dean. "Don't worry. You didn't do anything wrong."

Dean groaned. "I know, but this is still going to come back on me somehow. I just know it. We are talking about Matt Taylor, after all."

Andrew pursed his lips as he stared downstream. The creek bank was lined with nearly impassable bushes that were flooded with water. In fact, there didn't appear to be any solid ground in sight.

"They're never going to be able to pull into shore; there is no shore," Andrew said.

Dean looked downstream. "Well, surely the creek crosses another road somewhere."

Andrew shook his head. "I don't know. I only studied the map for as far as we were going to go. I think it cuts back across the 310 Highway somewhere, but that's halfway to the lake, about seven kilometers from here. Can you imagine how long it's going to take them to go seven kilometers with this stream winding back and forth the way it does?"

"So, they get out in the middle of some farmer's field

and walk home. Serves them right."

Andrew looked at Dean. "And then how do we pick up the canoe?"

"We? They got themselves into this mess. Let them figure it out. They can portage it, or whatever that word is."

"But it's my uncle's canoe."

"Oh yeah, right."

"It's too wet to drive into a field. In fact, I bet you half of the fields are flooded right now. Have you ever tried walking through a field when it's wet?" Andrew frowned as he stared downstream. "Matt! Chad!"

Both boys listened, but no reply came. Dean yelled their names again, louder this time, but there was still no answer. Andrew looked back at their canoe and then downstream.

"I think we should go after them," he said finally.

Dean stared at him. "What? Are you crazy? What good would that do? Then we'll all be in trouble. We should just wait here for your dad."

"I've got a hunch," Andrew said, "that the creek does cross a road not too far north of here, by Selkirk's pasture. Maybe we can put out there. It's probably only a kilometer's walk. We can be there and back within an hour."

"I don't think so. We're already way later than we said we would be. What's your dad going to do when he comes back and we're still not here? Let's just wait for him. He'll know what to do."

Andrew shook his head. "I don't know. They're not experienced canoeists. What if they get into trouble, run into some more rapids? They'll need help."

Dean took a step back off the bridge. "Okay, you want to help them? Go ahead. I'll stay here and wait for your dad. In fact, I'll walk home and let my parents know what's going on."

Andrew eyed the rushing water. "I don't know, Dean. I don't think I can handle the canoe by myself, especially if we get into some rough water."

Dean stared at the creek. He looked back toward town. There was no sign of any traffic on the road. He groaned and zipped up his life jacket. "Okay. I'll do it. But when we get in trouble—and I know we will—I'm telling my parents it was your idea."

"I'll take full responsibility," Andrew said. "I know you're only going along to help me—and Matt and Chad. You're a good friend, Dean."

Dean tried to frown but then finally broke into a grin. "Yeah, well, just remember this the next time I ask you for a favor."

"I will," Andrew said, already heading toward their canoe. "Now let's go!"

8

LAND HO!

It did not take long for Andrew and Dean to catch up with Matt and Chad. They paddled hard until they spotted the Taylor boys drifting along the shoreline looking for a place to get out.

Dean looked back at Andrew and put a finger to his lips. They boys remained silent until they were right behind Matt and Chad. Then Dean smacked his paddle on the water's surface, splashing the other two boys.

"Aaaggh!" Chad cried, cringing under the cold spray.

Matt whipped around, angry at first and then elated when he spotted Andrew and Dean. "I thought you were some kind of a rogue beaver!"

"You guys deserved that for making us go past the bridge!" Dean said. He splashed the boys again.

Matt grinned, undaunted by the fact he was soaked yet again. "I can't believe you guys followed us! We were just looking for a place to get out, but there's no solid ground anywhere. Even this snow," he stuck his paddle into a large snowdrift that was sandwiched between some shrubs, "it's just floating here, like a giant iceberg."

Andrew nodded. "I was afraid of that." He looked

around but could not see anything beyond the bushes, which formed a ten-foot wall above either side of the creek. "I think we can get out at Selkirk's pasture. It's not too far from here."

"Good idea," Matt said.

"Did you at least find the paddle?" Dean asked.

"Oh yeah." Matt reached down to the floor of the canoe and held it up. "Here it is!"

He tossed it over to Andrew. Andrew caught it in his free hand and then laid his plank in the bottom of his canoe.

"You can probably get rid of that old thing now," Dean said, glancing back.

Andrew shook his head. "You never know; it might come in handy later. We're not out of this yet."

"Good thinking," Matt said. "So, boys, should we continue on?"

"I guess so," Dean said. "But your parents are going to be really upset."

"Not half as upset as your mom is going to be," Matt replied. "Besides, once we tell them we were on a rescue mission, they'll be fine."

Dean scoffed. "That's what you think."

As the boys drifted downstream, every once in a while a hole opened up in the bushes, and they saw the low-lying areas all around them were flooded as well. There was no solid ground in sight, and they still had not seen any sign of the road near Selkirk's pasture.

"I had no idea there would be this much water on the prairies," Chad said.

"Neither did I," Andrew admitted. "Although I should have figured it out. My grandpa said he hasn't seen this much snow since he was a kid."

"Are you sure about your directions, Andrew?" Matt

asked, turning to look at him.

"Not really," Andrew said. He looked up at the sun. "We've been winding back and forth for a while now, but I think we're still heading roughly north. It's hard to get your bearings when there aren't any landmarks."

"What time is it?" Chad asked.

Andrew looked at his watch. "Twelve thirty."

"Boy, our parents are probably really wondering where we are," Matt said.

"We should have left a note at the bridge," Dean suggested. "My mom packed Jiffy markers and everything."

Andrew's ears reddened. "Yeah, I should have thought of that."

The boys fell silent as they continued to drift downstream. The creek was wide and deep, so they were not too worried about running into any obstacles, such as rapids, but much of their enthusiasm had dissipated. Not even Matt was excited about the prospect of a never-ending canoe trip. Like the other boys, he stared out at the landscape and wondered when the journey would end. Every once in a while, he tried to encourage the guys as they rounded a bend in the stream. "We're almost there! Just one more corner," he would say, but when all that appeared around the next bend was more water and more bushes, even he started to lose hope.

It did not help that the sun had receded behind a wall of scattered clouds. It peeked out occasionally and lit up the water and surrounding landscape with a cheery glow, but then it disappeared again, leaving everything looking even more faded and gloomier than before. A cool wind picked up, which only served to dampen the boys' mood further.

Matt rubbed his stomach. "I'm getting hungry."

"Me, too," Chad said.

Everyone was silent for a moment, and then all three boys looked at Dean. He held up his hands in self-defense.

"Don't look at me. I didn't tell you guys to dump your lunch in the river."

"Creek," Andrew said.

"Whatever!"

"For your information, Dean, Chad didn't dump his lunch in the creek; he ate it," Matt pointed out.

"Well, I can't help that," Dean said. "He should have packed more—or saved some for later."

The boys fell silent again.

"You know, we could be out here for a while," Andrew said a few moments later. "I don't think we should be arguing about food. If we don't find a way out of this soon, we're all going to need something to eat, just to keep up our strength."

"We should never have gone past the graveyard bridge," Dean said.

Chad and Matt lowered their eyes.

"Sorry, Dean," Matt said. "I guess I just got a little too excited."

Dean scoffed. "What else is new?"

"I didn't mean for anyone to get into trouble."

"Neither did I," Chad added.

Dean sighed. "I forgive you guys, but you'd better do some sweet talking to my parents for me when we get home—if we ever get back home. One thing I can tell you for sure: My mom is never going to let me go off on one of your hare-brained adventures again, Matt Taylor."

Matt, Chad, and Andrew each tried to suppress a smile, but Dean's freckled face was so serious they simply had to laugh.

"You sound just like your mom!" Matt exclaimed,

which only made the other boys laugh even harder.

Dean glared at them until he finally broke into a laugh as well. "I hate you guys."

"We love you, too, Dean," Matt replied.

"Speaking of food," Chad said, once the laughter had died down, "perhaps we can stop over there and have a snack." He pointed to a small, grassy hillock that was just coming up off to their left.

Matt raised his paddle in the air. "Land ho!"

Dean smiled. "At last!"

9

LEHMAN'S ISLAND

The boys' enthusiasm returned as they beached their canoes in a small inlet at the base of the hill and then scrambled up the grassy bank. When they reached the top of the hill, they realized they were in the middle of what used to be an old farmyard.

"Cool!" Matt said as he picked up the rusted blade of an old scythe. The wooden handle had long since rotted away.

The ruins of an old house sagged under the weight of time and decay. It was constructed of old, peeling logs. Although the frame remained intact, most of the roof had fallen in, and the entire structure was tilted toward one end, as if a strong wind had pushed it over. The windows were mostly broken, and the front door was nowhere to be seen. Strewn about the farmyard were all sorts of old, rusted farm implements, tin cans, barrels, rolls of barbed wire, smashed wooden crates, broken bottles and jars, and even an old pick-up truck. The truck looked like it was from the 1950s. It was shot through with weeds, and saplings poked out through the windows and holes in the rusted body.

As the boys wandered through the mess, they saw two

low outbuildings partially hidden by trees. Upon closer inspection, they concluded they were chicken coops. At least that's what they smelled like. Although the farm looked like it had not been occupied for decades, the buildings still gave off a slightly pungent odor. Like the house, the outbuildings were made from thick, rough-hewn logs with small, dark windows that were probably half a meter square. The roofs were made out of sod. A diverse mixture of grass, weeds, and even a few small trees had established themselves on top of the buildings over the years.

"Wow, I can't believe these old buildings are still standing" Matt said.

"They built things to last back then," Andrew observed.

Matt peeked inside the doorway and waited for his eyes to adjust to the gloom. A chicken roost, a couple of old buckets, and an old leather boot came into view. "I'm going inside for a closer look."

"Watch out for bats," Dean warned.

"There aren't any bats out here," Matt said. Then he paused and looked back at Andrew. "Are there?"

Andrew shrugged. "There might be. They do like old, abandoned buildings."

Matt turned to Chad. "On second thought, maybe you should go first."

"Forget it," Chad said. "Let's go check out the house."

"Sure," Matt agreed.

As the boys turned toward the house, Dean looked around at all of the trash strewn about the yard. "Imagine," he said. "This looks like a junk pile now, but at one point, this was somebody's home. I wonder who it was."

"If I knew where we were, I could check the RM map when we get home," Andrew said.

"No need to wait 'til then," Matt replied.

Dean and Andrew turned to where Matt was crouched outside the front door of the house. As the other boys walked over, Matt stood up and held out a small piece of paper. "Check this out"

It was a check, made out for $17.46. The name of the person to whom it was written was smudged, but the name of the person who wrote it was clear enough: Harold Lehman. The date on the check was July 21, 1972.

"Wow, someone was living here only thirteen years ago?" Matt glanced around. "It looks like this place has been abandoned for a hundred years!"

"The forest is a living thing," Andrew said. "Once you stop cutting it back, it isn't long until it takes over."

"Tell me about it. Hey guys, isn't that a road over there?"

Matt pointed past the truck. The boys peered at the bushes and could just make out a two-lane track stretching off into the forest. It was overgrown with trees, but it was definitely there.

"Looks like it," Chad said.

Matt looked at the other boys, his eyes alive with excitement. "You know what that means, right?"

"Where there's one road, there's bound to be another," Andrew replied, nodding. "The guy who lived here had to get in and out of here somewhere. Maybe we can follow it back to the highway."

"Let's go!" Matt said, already running toward it.

Their hunger forgotten, the boys charged off down the "road" to see where it would lead.

About two hundred meters into the woods, the road dipped down a hill and into a huge pool of water. It was fed by a small tributary that flowed into Milligan Creek. The pool was at least thirty meters across, and it looked quite deep. Worse, it stretched around to the boys' right—

away from the creek—and seemed to encircle the entire piece of land on which the farmyard stood. The boys stood by the water's edge and looked longingly toward the other side, where the track disappeared and then was choked off with trees.

"We could canoe across and see where the trail leads," Andrew suggested.

"And then what?" Matt asked. "Drag the canoes through the bush on the other side? Forget it. We don't even know if the highway is in that direction."

"This track has to lead to another road somewhere," Andrew insisted.

"We could just leave the canoes on the other side and walk out," Dean suggested. "And then come back and pick them up when the water goes down."

"It won't be any easier to get them out of here later than it is now," Matt said. "In fact, it'll be harder—harder than paddling them out, I mean."

Dean's shoulders sagged.

"Hey, don't give up, Dean," Andrew said. "We'll get out of here one way or another."

"Let's see if there's any way to walk around the far side of this pool," Andrew said.

The boys followed Andrew along the shoreline of the pool as it curved off to their right. The pool got wider as they walked. After a short while, it narrowed again, and soon the boys saw how the pool had formed in the first place.

"Beaver dam," Matt said. The boys watched as the water rushed over the dam, which had been overwhelmed by the flood.

"We're surrounded," Dean said. "Surrounded by water on all sides."

"You know what this means, don't you guys?" Matt said, his face brightening. "We're on an island, Lehman's Island."

Dean smiled. "I've never been on an island before. Cool."

"You bet it's cool," Matt said. "And you know there's only one way off an island, right?"

"By boat!" Dean and Chad replied in unison. Then they looked over at Andrew and grinned.

"Or canoe," Andrew said, smiling.

"Right," Matt said. "So let's go back and have something to eat. After that, we'll hit the road, er, I mean, the water!"

Excited about the adventure once again, the boys ran back through the trees toward the farmyard.

The shadows were already starting to slant somewhat in the mid-afternoon sun, but the boys were able to find a nice warm, sunny spot overlooking the water, where they could have a quick bite. Dean unpacked his knapsack, and soon the boys were all lying around munching on crackers, beef jerky, chocolate chip oatmeal cookies, and granola bars. At Andrew's suggestion, they saved some of the food for later, just in case. Dean and Chad also passed around their water bottles.

When they were done, Matt lay back on the grass, laced his hands behind his head, closed his eyes, and tilted his face toward the sun.

"Man, Dean, your mom packed enough food for an army." He yawned. "With all that food in my belly, I sure could go for a nap. What time is it, Andrew?"

Andrew pulled up the sleeve of his sweatshirt so he could see his watch. "Two thirty."

"Hmph. Feels way later than that." Matt rolled onto his side. "How long have we been on this journey?"

"About six hours now, since we left your house anyway," Andrew said.

"I just wonder how many more hours 'til it's over,"

Dean said.

"Hopefully not too long," Chad replied. "I want to get home in time to watch the Oilers game tonight."

"If we're not grounded," Matt pointed out.

"Which you will be," Dean said.

Chad sat up. "I never thought of that. Maybe we'd better get moving."

He and the other boys rose to their feet, reluctant to leave the tranquil spot but eager to continue the journey.

A few minutes later, the boys were back at the canoes. Matt was the last one to descend the grassy bank. He turned back for one last look at the farmyard.

"Goodbye, Lehman Island. Don't know when we'll be back, but it was fun while it lasted."

He was about to slide down the bank when something caught his eye. "Just a second, guys."

He ran off to investigate. Moments later he reappeared at the top of the knoll. "Hey guys, look!"

Andrew, Chad, and Dean looked up as Matt hefted an old, tan crock, a ceramic container in which people used to store flour and sugar and other food items. The crock looked like it would hold about five gallons. It was so heavy Matt could barely lift it.

"Cool," Dean said. "Where'd you find it?"

"Behind some bushes over there."

"Any more of them?" Dean asked. "My mom would love to have one. Maybe if I gave her one, that would take a week or two off my grounding."

Matt shook his head. "Just some broken pieces. This was the only good one, and even it has a crack in it." He turned it around so Dean could see.

"Too bad," Dean said.

"Hey Matt, you can't take that," Chad pointed out as

Matt started to descend toward the canoes.

"Why not?" Matt asked, stopping.

"Because it doesn't belong to you."

"Aw, come on, Chad. Nobody's been here for years."

"Someone still owns this land," Andrew pointed out. "And whoever owns the land owns that crock, too."

Matt eyed the crock longingly, knowing the other boys were right but looking for some way to keep it anyway. "Maybe, but they're never going to miss it. Besides, if we show up back home with this, at least one of our moms will be less likely to kill us."

"Exactly," Dean said. "We can draw straws for it."

Andrew shook his head. "I don't know . . ."

"What if we track down Mr. Lehman's relatives and see if they want it? If not, we draw straws like Dean said to see whose mom gets it."

Chad glanced at Andrew. He shrugged. "Sounds good to me."

Matt slid down the bank, careful not to damage the crock. He was about to set it in his and Andrew's canoe when he slipped on the wet grass and tumbled forward. The crock flew out of his hands and landed right in the canoe.

"Are you okay?" Chad asked as he stood up to help his brother.

"I think so," Matt said, standing up and wiping himself off. "Is the crock okay?"

"Yeah, but now we have bigger problems." Andrew said, staring at the bottom of the canoe.

"What do you mean?" Matt asked, leaning forward.

Andrew pulled the crock aside, revealing a small fountain of water bubbling into the canoe through a hairline crack in the floor.

"Uh oh." Matt looked up at Andrew. "Sorry, Andy. I can't imagine your uncle is going to be too happy about that."

Andrew shoved the crock aside. "It's not my uncle I'm worried about. How are we going to get home in a leaky canoe?"

Matt's face went serious. "I didn't think of that." Then an idea struck him. "Hey, Dean, you got any gum?"

"Yeah, why?"

"Just give it to me."

Dean dug in his pack and handed Matt a stick.

"No, not one stick, the whole pack."

Dean frowned. "What? How come?"

"Just do it!"

With a sigh, Dean pulled out the pack of gum and tossed it to Matt. Matt unwrapped the pieces, jamming them into his mouth as he did. He chewed furiously for a few minutes and then spit the wet, pink glob into his hand. He wiped his mouth and grinned at the other boys.

"One canoe patch, coming up!"

Andrew shook his head skeptically. "I don't know about that."

A minute later, Matt had spread the gum over the crack, reducing the leak to a slow dribble.

"I doubt it'll last long," Andrew said, "but even if it doesn't, I suppose we can always bail the water out. It's only a slow leak."

"Exactly," Matt said, scooping an old tobacco can out of the bushes to use as a bailing can. "Now let's go! Chad has a hockey game to watch, after all."

"Yeah right," Dean said. "When you guys get home, you're going to be grounded from TV for the rest of your lives."

"That's okay," Matt said. "It just leaves us more time to plan adventures like this."

Dean groaned. "On second thought, maybe your parents should punish you by forcing you to stay inside and watch TV. Destroy a few of those insane brain cells of yours."

The other boys laughed as they pushed off.

"Goodbye, Lehman Island," Matt called as the current drew them away.

"Good riddance!" Dean said.

A few moments later, the lonely farmyard disappeared from view, and the boys set their minds on the next stage of their journey.

10

Sailing the "Ocean" Blue

The current was swift and strong for the first while, and the boys made good time. But soon the creek began to twist and turn, and the boys had to work hard to maneuver around each bend, often ducking to avoid overhanging branches. They were surrounded by flooded clumps of willow and alder bushes with no solid ground in sight. Every once in a while a gap opened up, but the boys could see nothing but more flooded bushes beyond.

After twisting back and forth for a time, they came to a fork in the creek. The current was terribly sluggish, but the boys still had to paddle into a clump of bushes to stop themselves while they decided which way to go. Matt took the opportunity to bail some water out of the canoe. His feet were sloshing around in about two inches of the wet stuff. Chad leaned back and stretched his back. Like the other boys, his muscles were tired and achy from sitting and paddling all day.

"So, which way, Andrew?" Dean asked.

Andrew shook his head. "I don't know." He looked up at the sun and pointed to their left. "I think that's south, but I'm not sure. The sun's supposed to follow a more southerly path in the sky at this time of year, but the creek has twisted back and forth so many times I don't know which way is up. Anyway, we want to go north. But it's hard to tell which of these branches goes that way."

"Maybe they both link up again later on," Chad suggested.

"Maybe," Andrew said. "I guess it doesn't really matter which one we take. They're both going to come to a road sooner or later."

"You hope," Dean said.

"Okay, so how should we decide?" Chad asked. "By vote?"

"Sure," Andrew said.

"All right, whoever wants to go right, hold up your paddle," Matt said.

No one made a move.

"Okay, how about left?" Matt held up his paddle, but no one else did. "What's the matter with you guys?" Matt asked. "Andrew said it doesn't matter."

"Just a second, Matt," Andrew said. "I don't know why, but something tells me we should go right."

"Okay, then right it is." Matt pushed away from the tree. "Anything to get a move on."

"Are you sure, Andrew?" Chad asked as he eyed the creek warily.

"Pretty sure."

Just then, a gust of wind billowed through an opening in the bushes, sending a chill through the boys.

Dean shivered. "Well, I guess we can't just sit here. Let's go, Chad."

Over the next hour, the boys had to paddle constantly to keep their canoes moving. Matt looked down at his feet. The water was seeping in faster than before, the gum long gone. He lifted his feet up onto the bow plate to keep them out of the icy bath while he bailed as fast as he could.

The wind picked up a little more, whipping up small wavelets on the surface of the otherwise tranquil creek.

"It's starting to get cold already," Dean said as he hunched under his life jacket. "Sure could use some of those extra clothes about now." He glared at Matt.

"Hey, that gives me an idea," Andrew said. "Come on over here, you guys."

Chad and Dean paddled their canoe over until they came up alongside Andrew and Matt.

"What's up?" Chad asked.

"Let me see those towels," Andrew said, gesturing to Dean's pack.

"Sure." Dean reached back to undo the straps. "But they're kind of wet."

"That doesn't matter. In fact, if my plan works, we'll have them dry in no time."

Now the other boys were really curious. Dean pulled the towels out of his backpack and tossed them over to Andrew. Andrew grabbed the plank he had used for a paddle and stood it up in front of him.

"Hold onto the gunnels for a minute to steady the canoe, Matt."

Matt did as he was told. Once Andrew was standing, he took one corner of Dean's towel, stuck it through a knothole in the wood, and then brought it out the other side and tied a knot. Then he took the other corner of the towel, stretched it as far as it would go, and tried to tie it around the other end of the board. It would not quite reach. He looked over at Dean.

"Dean, do you have any safety pins in your First Aid kit?"

"I think so." Dean rooted through his knapsack until he came up with a small, yellow, cylindrical nylon bag with a red cross on the side.

"Cool, where'd you get that?" Matt asked.

"My cousin, Dave, worked on the fire crew up north last year. He went to university in the fall and didn't need it anymore, so he gave it to me." Dean unzipped the bag and emptied its contents into his lap. It contained Band-Aids, antiseptic wipes, a small pair of scissors, cloth bandages, and, finally, safety pins.

"Here you go." Dean leaned over to the other canoe. "There's six of them. Hope that's enough."

"That's plenty," Andrew said. "Thanks."

Andrew put the safety pins in his mouth. Then he wound the towel tightly around the board again and pinned it in place. "Perfect. Here, Matt, hold this."

Andrew held the board out for Matt to take. Once Matt had it, Andrew bent down and picked up his paddle. Then he took the other end of the towel and attached it to the paddle the same way he had attached it to the board.

Just then, a gust of wind rocked the canoes, and the boys paused for a moment to steady themselves. A light flashed in Matt's eyes.

"I get it," he said. "You're making a sail!"

Andrew grinned through his mouthful of safety pins but said nothing. Once he was done attaching the towel, he held out his hand toward Dean. "Your paddle? I'll also need that other towel."

After Dean handed the items over to him, Andrew attached the second towel to the piece of wood and Dean's paddle. Then he handed the paddle back to Dean. The boys each held a paddle while the piece of wood stood straight up in the middle, a towel tied to either side. "Okay, we've got a sail. Now we need to attach the canoes. Chad, you've got some rope tied to the stern of your canoe back there. Is it long enough to tie the two canoes together?"

Chad fished the yellow nylon rope up out of the water behind him. "Yep, it's long enough." He set down his paddle, reached for the stern of Andrew and Matt's boat, and pulled them together so he could begin tying.

Andrew turned to Matt. "You do the same thing up in the bow."

"Already on it," Matt replied. He grunted as he leaned over the bow and pulled the rope out of the water.

Once the canoes were tied together, Andrew took the board and wedged it between the canoes. Then he took off his life jacket, laid it across the gunnels of both canoes, and sat down, holding what was now their mast.

"Okay, Matt and Dean, you guys will need to hold the paddles out to the sides as far as you can. I'll hold onto the mast, and Chad will steer by putting his paddle in the water and using it as a rudder. Everybody got it?"

"Got it!" the boys replied.

Matt and Dean moved into place and held out the paddles. The sail wasn't very big, but the wind caught it immediately and puffed out the towels, twisting the canoes to the left.

"Put your paddle in the water, Chad," Andrew said, looking up to make sure the safety pins would hold. "If you want to make the canoe go left, turn your paddle to the right. If you want to go right, turn your paddle to the left. Got it?"

Chad held his paddle above the water while he went through the motions and repeated the commands quietly to himself. "To go left, turn right, to go right, turn left." He looked up at Andrew. "Got it!" Then he put his paddle in the water. A moment later, the canoes started turning back to the right.

"It's working!" Matt exclaimed. "Look down at the water, we're actually moving!"

91

The boys looked down and saw tiny waves cascading out from either side of their canoes.

"Now we can get some rest," Chad said as he leaned forward and peered beneath the sail so he could see where they were going.

"Speak for yourself," Dean said through clenched teeth. "This is harder than rowing."

"Paddling," Andrew said.

"Whatever!"

Andrew looked at his watch. "Don't worry, Dean. One of us will trade off with Chad every ten minutes. That way none of us will get too tired."

"Make it every five," Dean said. "I mean it."

"Five it is," Andrew said. "You can rest first."

The boys sailed on like that for the next half hour. Although, like Dean said, it was not much easier than paddling, they enjoyed the fact they had been able construct their own form of locomotion. They passed the time by telling jokes and singing songs they had learned at summer camp the year before.

"Down by the bay," Matt sang.

"Down by the bay," the others echoed.

"Where the watermelons grow,"

"Where the watermelons grow,"

"Back to my home,"

"Back to my home,"

"I dare not go."

"I dare not go."

"For if I do,"

"For if I do,"

"My mother will say,"

"My mother will say,"

"Your turn, Dean," Matt said.

Dean smiled. "Did you ever see Jaws eating women's

92

bras?"

Everyone stopped and stared at him.

"What?" Dean asked. "It rhymes."

The other boys laughed and then chimed in. "Down by the bay, down by the bay!"

As the other boys continued to sing, Chad, who was holding Dean's paddle on the right side of the sail, looked up at the sky with concern. "Uh, guys, did anyone else notice something?"

Matt, who was holding the mast, looked up at the sails as well. "Yeah, I guess I was too busy singing to think about it, but the towels sure aren't billowing out like they used to. So what? We'll go back to paddling."

"That's not what I meant," Chad said. "Listen."

The boys all fell silent for a moment. A few seconds later, they heard a distant rumble.

"Is that thunder?" Matt asked.

"In spring?" Dean said. "We never get thunderstorms in the spring."

"Never say never," Andrew said.

The boys scanned the sky as they continued to listen, but apart from a few dark clouds on the horizon, there was no further sign—or sound—of a storm.

Andrew lowered his side of the sail. "Thunder or no thunder, we should get paddling again. Otherwise we're never going to get out of here." He looked up at the sun, which was already beginning its descent across the sky.

"Well, it was fun while it lasted," Matt said as he unpinned the towels. "And look, Big Bird is all dry!"

The boys quickly dismantled the sail and got back into their seats.

"Hey, I just got an idea," Matt said.

"What's that?" Andrew asked.

"Why don't we keep the canoes tied together like this?

It's more fun than being on our own. Plus, it's more stable. We can even get up and walk around. See?" He stood up and tried to rock the canoes, but they hardly moved.

"Good idea," Andrew said. "It'll also make it easier for your dad to spot us from the air."

At the mention of their parents, the boys fell silent. It only reminded them of the grim welcome that was awaiting them when—and if—they made it home.

After a few moments, Matt looked up at the sky. "You'd think he'd be out looking for us by now."

"Maybe they're searching on the section of the creek that goes through town," Chad said. "Maybe they think we got into some kind of trouble."

The boys grew quiet once again as the gravity of the situation dawned on them. For all they knew, their parents were frantically searching the creek, fearing the worst. It might not even have occurred to them yet that the boys had actually gone beyond the bridge.

Of all the boys, Dean's face showed the most concern. His skin went pale behind his freckles, making the tiny brown specks stand out even more. He hung his head between his knees and gripped it with his hands.

"I never should have listened to you guys," he said. "My mom's probably worried sick. And my dad . . . I think I'd be better off dying out here than going home."

"Don't be ridiculous," Matt said. "It's not your fault. We'll take all the blame."

"That's right," Chad said. "Won't we, Andrew?"

Andrew nodded grimly. "Right." His eyes appeared to be fixated on some point in his mind, most likely his parents' reaction to their disappearance.

"Thanks, guys, but I don't think it's going to make a difference," Dean said. "They already think you're nothing but trouble. Well, you anyway, Matt."

"Aw, come off it, Dean, your parents love me."

Dean did not reply.

"I think we need to forget about getting in trouble and focus more on getting home," Chad said. "We owe our parents that much at least. They were nice enough to let us go on this trip, and now we've really blown it. They're probably worried sick about us, and it's our duty to get out of here as soon as possible so we can let them know we're all right."

"You're right, Chad," Matt said. "We've just been thinking about ourselves. It's time to start thinking about them." He held his paddle up in the air. "Ready to paddle boys?"

"Let's do it!" Dean said. At that, they all dug their paddles deep into the water and pulled forward. It was a little choppy at first, but then they fell into a good rhythm.

"Stroke! Stroke! Stroke!" Matt called out to keep them in sync. Soon they were gliding through the water and making good time.

A short while later, they noticed the creek was beginning to open up somewhat. In the distance, they saw a break in the trees, which were taller now, and they wondered if they were finally coming to a road. The boys paddled with renewed vigor, spurred on by hope. But as they drew closer to the opening, they realized they were not approaching a road at all. In fact, it was anything but.

"What the heck?" Matt exclaimed.

"It's like the creek just ends," Chad said.

"In a lake," Dean added.

"We haven't gone all the way to Stony Lake, have we, Andrew?" Chad asked.

Andrew shook his head, his brow furrowed. "Not a chance. Let's keep paddling and see what's up."

The boys kept going until they reached the opening.

Then they all stopped at once, unable to believe their eyes. As they looked out, there was nothing but water and clumps of bushes for as far as the eye could see—which was not particularly far. But whatever the case, the creek was gone. It had turned into a flood plain. Directly ahead of the boys was a large hill, which rose up about thirty meters out of the water. The bottom of the hill was covered in scrub bush and small poplar trees, but the crest of the hill merely sported a thin covering of dead grass, which waved back and forth in the breeze. The slanting rays of the sun made the top of the hill glow a friendly, golden color.

"A lookout point!" Andrew said. "Maybe we can finally figure out where the heck we are."

"Let's paddle, boys!" Matt replied.

He need not have bothered, because the others had already started pulling for the shore, driven more by their aching muscles than anything else.

11

A GOOD SIGN

It did not take long for the boys to reach the base of the hill. They paddled hard over the final few meters and then lifted their paddles out of the water so the canoes would drive themselves onto the shore as far as possible. None of them were too excited about getting their feet wet at that point in the day.

"Come on," Matt said, his right foot already on shore. "We'd better get up there before we lose our light."

The other boys scrambled out and started up the hill.

"Hold on a second," Dean said after running a few steps. He bent down to touch his toes. "My back is killing me."

"It's all that sitting on the cold metal seat," Andrew said as he bent down to touch his own toes. "It's good to stretch it out, just like you're doing."

"Will you old ladies come on?" Matt said.

He turned and disappeared into the woods. Dean rolled his eyes and then turned to follow. Andrew smiled as he brought up the rear. Chad kept pace with Matt.

It was a steep climb, but the boys finally emerged out of the woods and into the tall grass and thistles, which clawed at their pant legs. Matt was the first to reach the top of the hill, followed closely by Chad. The two of them stood and stared as Andrew and Dean crossed the final stretch of ground to join them. When they reached the top, Andrew and Dean also stood aghast at the view.

Andrew was the first one to break the silence. "I can't believe it."

"We must have taken a wrong turn back there somewhere," Matt said.

"Tell me about it," Chad replied.

The boys scanned the world below them. It was the first time they were really able to take a good look at the ground they had covered in the past several hours. To their amazement, they saw that the hill was an island in the middle of a lake of water that stretched a kilometer or more in every direction. Despite their predicament, the boys could not help but be amazed at the beauty of it all. The reflection of the sun's fading rays as they glinted off the wind-rippled water only served to heighten their sense of awe.

After a few moments, Matt finally asked the question that had been burning in all of their minds. "How the heck are we going to get out of this?"

"Well, at least we finally have a fairly good idea of bearings now," Andrew said. "Let's see, if that's west—where the sun's going down—then that's north. Hmm . . .."

He turned back to look at the direction from which they had just come. He could just faintly make out the snaking line of the stream as it wound its way back into a maze of bushes and trees. He turned south and saw the grain elevators and the lights of Milligan Creek just beginning to wink on in the distance. Behind the town was a tall, nasty looking bank of dark clouds, but Andrew and the other boys were too intent on finding their way home to notice.

He turned back to face the north again and scanned the distant shoreline. "Okay, guys, I think I might have an idea where we are."

"Oh yeah, Christopher Columbus? Where?" Matt asked.

Andrew looked at him. "Remember the community pasture we visited last year to take a look at that herd of buffalo?"

The other boys nodded. Andrew pointed down at the ground below. "Well, I think this is it."

"Really?" Dean stared at the water all around them. "I don't see any buffalo."

"Of course not, dummy," Matt said.

"No, what I mean is—"

"If I remember correctly, the pasture manager's house is located on a ridge somewhere along the north side of the pasture," Andrew said. "And if I'm not mistaken, that's the ridge over there." He pointed to the northern shore of the lake. "Can anyone see it?"

The boys were silent for a moment as they scanned the ridge. It was covered with several thick stands of poplar broken up by more pasture land.

"There it is!" Dean said. The boys looked in the direction he was pointing. Seconds later they were all jumping up and down.

"We're saved!"

"Okay, let's get back to the canoes," Matt said as he turned and loped off down the hill.

"Wait a minute," Andrew said.

Matt stopped. "What's up, Andy?"

Andrew turned and looked back toward the community pasture manager's farm. "Things look pretty clear from up here. But once we get back down into those bushes again, it'll be easy to lose our way. I just want to pick out a few landmarks to make sure we don't wind up paddling in circles."

"Good idea," Matt said, walking back to join Andrew.

"Okay, there's that dead poplar tree sticking up from that clump of bushes over there," Andrew said as he pointed to it. "That'll be our first landmark."

"Got it," Matt said.

"Hmm . . . after that, I don't really see anything tall enough for us to see from down on the water."

"Can't we just make sure the dead tree is always behind us?" Dean asked.

"It'll look like it's behind you no matter what direction you go from it," Andrew said.

"Oh," Dean replied. "I didn't think about that."

"That's okay," Andrew said. "I think I can see a path. All we have to do is remember to keep slanting to our right once we pass the tree. It's not too far from there to that strip of open water between the bushes and the shore. Even if we go a little bit off course, we'll be all right. It'll just mean a bit of extra paddling."

"Are you sure?" Chad asked. "Won't we wind up going in a circle if we keep heading right?"

Andrew turned and examined their course one last time and then shook his head. "I don't think so. We'll be okay."

"Then let's go!" Matt said.

"One second," Chad said.

"What now?" Matt asked, turning back again.

"Take a look over there. Doesn't that look like a row of grain bins to you?"

Chad pointed down the shore to the east. The boys all stood and stared, but no one could make out what Chad was seeing.

"Probably just a hallucination," Matt said. "Too much paddling, not enough food."

"Maybe," Chad said, still unconvinced.

"Forget about it, Chad," Matt said, clapping his brother's back. "We've already found a farmyard. Let's go!"

With that, the boys tore off down the hill, running and whooping the entire way down.

As they neared the canoes, the boys slowed to a walk. Now that the end of the journey was in sight, they were beginning to reflect back on the day's events.

"This has been some adventure," Matt said. "Way better than I ever thought it would be."

"It has been pretty interesting," Andrew admitted.

"Not to mention scary," Dean added.

"After all we've been through, I'm sure glad your mom packed all of that extra stuff," Chad said.

"Yeah, I'll never make fun of you or your mom again," Matt said. "Or you. Sorry, Dean."

Dean smiled. "No problem. I'm just glad it all worked out."

"Not yet it hasn't," Andrew reminded them.

Just then the boys heard what sounded like a large animal crashing through the bushes off to their right. They froze on the spot.

"A bear!" Dean yelled, already searching for a tree to climb. However, the poplar trees only started sprouting climbable branches about twenty feet in the air.

"I don't think so," Andrew whispered. "But stay still just in case."

"Could it be one of those buffalo?" Chad asked.

"It would be a water buffalo by now," Matt said, and chuckled. Chad joined in until Andrew shushed them again.

"Look," Andrew said. At that moment, about twenty meters to their right, a fawn trotted out of the woods and sniffed the air. It had white spots along its side. The rest of its body was covered in a fine coat of ruddy brown hair. A moment later, its mother appeared.

"It's beautiful," Dean whispered.

The fawn started at the sound and then turned and dashed off into the trees. The boys relaxed and started walking toward the canoes again.

"I'll take that as a good sign," Chad said.

"Good enough for me," Matt replied. "Now, let's get the heck out of here before one of those buffalo really does show up!"

The boys laughed as they ran toward the canoes.

12

DEAN MAKES A FRIEND

"I really think you should leave that crock behind," Andrew said as he helped Matt pull their canoe onshore and dump out the water.

"But we've already carried it so far. What good is it going to do way out here?" Matt asked as he set down his end of the canoe. "Besides, like I said, maybe it'll help to smooth things over if I bring mom a gift."

"A stolen gift? I don't think so," Chad said.

"Yeah, you'll probably get us into even more trouble," Dean said.

Matt hesitated as he stared down at the crock. It was wet and mud-spattered, and there was a big crack down one side. It didn't look nearly as nice as when he first discovered it. After a few moments, he picked it up and carried it over to the base of a tree.

"Maybe the pasture manager will find it one day," Matt said. "It'll be a cool discovery."

"If not, the cows can always drink from it when it fills up with rainwater," Chad said.

"Or the buffalo," Dean added.

Matt smiled. "Okay. Now let's get out of here."

Once again the boys set out on what they hoped would be the last leg of their trip.

Navigating through the clumps of bushes was not as difficult as they thought. They made straight for the tall, dead poplar tree, and soon they were able to catch glimpses of the far shore through gaps in the bushes ahead.

As they passed the dead tree, a hawk alighted on one of its uppermost branches and eyed the boys curiously. It tilted its head to one side and let out a shrill cry. Dean mimicked the bird's posture and tried to answer it in its own language. A moment later, the hawk gave out another cry and then flew away.

"Guess you must have said something to offend it," Matt said.

"Guess so," Dean said. "But it sure is beautiful."

"I think it's a red-tailed hawk," Andrew said as he watched it disappear into the sinking sun. "Must have just returned from down south. They're fairly rare around here."

"How do you know all this stuff?" Matt asked.

"I don't know, I guess I just read a lot," Andrew said as he dipped his paddle into the water. "Keep your eyes open. Evening is a great time to spot wildlife, especially around water. That's when they feed."

The boys kept their eyes and ears open, but they didn't see anything but a few ducks, which burst out from beneath the bushes and launched their round bodies into the air as the boys approached. Several flocks of geese also sailed by overhead in V-formation. Andrew explained that they were coming in to land on the water for the night so they would be safe from foxes, coyotes, and other predators.

A short while later, the boys emerged into the expanse of open water. All that remained between them and the shore, which was now about a kilometer away, were some small hummocks of grass poking up out of the water. The boys were amazed by the beauty of the sky and its reflection in the sun-dappled water as they paddled across the final stretch. A fairly strong wind had whipped up, and the boys were starting to feel chilled, but that did not bother them now that they were so close to their destination.

Just then, a low rumble echoed across the sky. This time there was no mistaking it.

"Thunder!" Dean cried.

The boys looked behind them just as the wind whipped up, tousling their hair. A towering mass of dark clouds had crept up behind them. As they stared at it in horror, lightning forked across the sky, followed almost immediately by another rumble.

"Paddle!" Andrew yelled.

The boys dug in and paddled for all their might as raindrops began to dapple the water around them and spatter their clothes.

Lightning flashed again, illuminating the air around them.

"We're all gonna die!" Dean cried.

"No we're not!" Matt said as he grit his teeth. "Keep paddling!"

"And stay low!" Andrew added.

After a long, hard paddle, the boys finally reached the shore. They leaped out of their canoes and then lay down on the ground, gasping as the rain poured down on their sweaty faces.

"That was a close one," Matt said.

"Tell me about it," Chad replied.

Right on cue, the sky lit up.

Andrew counted silently, his eyes on the sky. A few seconds later, thunder rumbled.

"Five seconds, between the lightning and the thunder," Andrew said. "It's already moving on."

After resting for a moment, the boys pulled their canoes completely out of the water in case it rose even further. They were just finishing up when they heard a familiar sound—a dog barking.

The boys looked up. At the top of the ridge was a large German shepherd. It berated the boys with its deep, throaty barks, and it looked rather menacing in the fading light.

Dean took a step back toward the canoes. "I don't know if this is such a good idea, guys."

Just then, the land was illuminated by another flash of lightning, followed by a menacing rumble.

"On second thought . . .." Dean edged away from the water.

He and the other boys watched as the dog barked two more times and then tore down the hill toward them.

"It's okay, Dean," Chad said as he stepped forward to meet the animal. "He's just a watchdog doing his job. I bet he's glad to see us. Especially in this storm."

Chad walked forward a few paces and crouched down to the dog's level. The dog stopped a few feet from him, sniffed the air, and then crept forward the last few paces. Chad held out his right hand, curling his fingers under, and offered the back of his wrist for the dog to sniff. The dog trotted up, sniffed Chad's hand, and then charged in and licked Chad's face.

"See? Nothing to be afraid of," Matt said, visibly relaxing a little.

"You can never be too careful," Dean said. "I don't trust strange dogs."

"Probably because they don't trust strange people, people like—" Matt stopped short when he saw Chad scowling at him. "Uh, you know, strange people like me."

"Exactly," Dean said.

Matt and Andrew stepped up to introduce themselves to the dog, but after one quick sniff, it bounded past them to greet Dean. Shocked by the sudden movement, Dean lost his balance and fell backwards, right into the canoe. The dog hesitated for a second and then took two bounding steps and leapt in after him.

"Aagghh!" Dean's muffled cry came from beneath the dog. He finally managed to pull himself away from the excited mutt, who was licking him furiously. The dog bounded up to the bow of the canoe and put his front paws on the seat. The other boys nearly doubled over with laughter at the sight.

"I think he likes you, Dean!" Chad said.

"Yeah, love at first sight," Matt added.

"Maybe he wants you to take him on a trip," Andrew suggested.

Dean couldn't help but smile. "I don't know about him, but I've had my fill of canoeing for now."

As Dean sat up, the dog leaped out of the canoe and then gave himself a hard shake, his coat wet from the rain, which was already beginning to slacken. The dog proceeded to jump and nip playfully at the boys as they turned the canoes over and stowed their paddles and life jackets underneath.

The boys were in great spirits as they made their way up the hill toward the farmyard. The rain had all but stopped, and two yard lights illuminated a cluster of red buildings in the graying sunset. The boys heard cattle down below in a pasture to their right. All seemed right with the world.

As the boys drew near to the farmhouse, however, their enthusiasm dimmed when the saw all of the windows were dark.

"Maybe they just ran into town," Matt said, always

the optimist.

As they approached the house, their worst fears were confirmed. No one was home. The dog ran over to his food dish, which was located next to the front door, and started eating voraciously. The dish was nothing more than an old hubcap heaped with dry dog biscuits. The boys knocked several times on the door just in case someone was inside. When they didn't get an answer, they tried the door handle. It was locked.

"What do we do now?" Dean asked as he looked around the farmyard.

"We wait, I guess," Andrew replied.

The exhausted boys sat down on the front stoop and dug into the last of Dean's food. The dog came over to join them. He plunked himself next to Dean and laid his head on his lap. His eyes looked up imploringly as Dean munched his last chocolate chip cookie. Dean tried to ignore the animal, but when he had only one bite left, he gave in and handed it to him.

"Love at first bite," Matt quipped.

"Looks like you're stuck with him," Chad added.

Dean reached down and ruffled the dog's fur. "Aw, he's not all that bad I guess."

Andrew looked at his watch. It was nearly 7:00, and it was completely dark, aside from the yard light. He stood up and stretched. "Think I'm going to take a look around," he said. "Can I borrow your flashlight, Dean?" Dean fished a small mag light out of his backpack. He switched it on and tossed it to Andrew.

"I'll come with you," Matt said. He leapt to his feet and dusted off his pants.

"Me too," Chad said as he got up.

"Me three," Dean added.

With that, the four boys and the dog set out to explore

the farmyard. Shivering from the cold and their damp clothing, they rubbed their hands together for warmth. They tried the door handle on each building in case one of them was open. It would be better to sit inside and wait than endure the cold outside. At least they would be out of the wind. No such luck.

One of the buildings was a storage shed, the second a pump house, and a third was some sort of garage or shop. As the boys shone the flashlight through the dusty windows, they saw that the far wall was lined with a long, greasy workbench that was littered with tools and partially disassembled machinery.

As the boys reached the final building—a lopsided, wooden structure located about ten meters from the house—they shone the flashlight in the window and were greeted immediately by a blaze of light reflecting off chrome.

"Wow, a Suburban," Matt exclaimed. "And it looks brand new!"

"You'd never know these guys had money judging from the shape of this yard," Dean said.

"You can never judge a book by its cover," Chad reminded him.

Dean shrugged. "I guess not."

Andrew tried the side door of the garage. It was locked. The boys walked around to the front of the garage and tried to open the double doors. They were locked, too.

"Now what are we going to do?" Dean asked, glancing around at the spooky, shadowy farmyard. "We can't sit out here all night; we'll freeze to death."

"When do you suppose they'll come home, Andrew?" Chad asked.

Andrew shrugged. "Who knows? Maybe they went out for supper."

"Or maybe they're away on a vacation and won't be back for two weeks," Dean said, his mind leaping automatically to the worst-case scenario.

"And leave the dog here on its own?" Matt shook his head. "I doubt it."

"The neighbors could be feeding it," Andrew suggested. Just then a thought occurred to all of the boys at once.

"Neighbors!" They shouted in unison.

"Let's go see if we can spot any other yard lights from the end of their driveway," Matt said.

The boys tore off down the rutted track that served as a road into the place. The dog ran along ahead of them, excited by all of the action. Andrew shone the flashlight ahead so they could see where they were going. The moon was starting to come up as well. It peeked in and out of the clouds, adding some extra illumination to the inky night as the boys ran down the forest-lined road.

Matt was the first one to spot it, and when he did, he stopped dead. Chad, who was right behind him, nearly plowed right into him. Andrew and Dean slowed down as they jogged up and then also came to a sudden stop.

In front of the boys, not ten meters away, was a huge pool of water. The driveway dipped down and was completely submerged under what looked to be about four or five feet of water. Andrew shone the flashlight across the expanse, and the boys spotted a canoe beached on the other side.

"So that's why the dog was so happy to see us," Dean said, scratching the pooch behind the ears. "Probably no one has been here for the past couple of days."

"We don't know that for sure, Dean," Chad said. "Just because they're flooded out doesn't mean they aren't still staying here."

Andrew turned the flashlight away from the canoe and

glanced up at the sky. "Well, whatever the case, we've got to find some shelter soon. We may have to spend the night."

"Spend the night?" Dean asked. "Oh man, my parents are going to *kill* me."

"Maybe we should try and break into the house and use the phone," Matt said. "We can always pay them back for the damage."

Andrew shook his head. "If one of us was in trouble, I'd do it. But no one's life is at stake. We're here because of our own stupidity. I think we're just going to have to lump it."

"But what about our parents?" Matt asked. "They're probably dragging the creek for our bodies right now."

"I don't know," Andrew said as they turned back toward the farmyard. "The chances of both canoes and all four of us disappearing in Milligan Creek are pretty slim. I'll bet they've figured out we went too far and marooned ourselves somewhere."

"I still can't figure out why we haven't seen Dad fly over in his plane," Matt said.

"Maybe because they didn't figure out what happened to us until it was too late," Chad suggested. "Remember, Dad can't fly after dark."

"Maybe," Matt said.

The boys turned and headed back to the house.

"Can't we try and canoe down the shore a ways to see if anyone else lives around here?" Dean asked. "Chad, didn't you see some grain bins farther down?"

Chad shrugged. "I thought so, but I'm not sure. Besides, just because there are bins there doesn't mean someone's living there. They might be flooded out, too. Or the bins may just be out in their field."

Dean's shoulders sagged.

Chad put a comforting hand on his friend's back.

"We'll definitely go check them out in the morning."

Matt clapped his hands together. "So, where are we going to spend the night, boys? Maybe we should make a fire."

"I have an idea," Andrew said. He looked over at Dean. "But I'll need your help."

"Me?" Dean asked. "What can I do?"

"You'll see," Andrew said. "Chad, I'll need you and Matt to help me as well."

"Sure thing," Chad said.

Andrew led the way over to the building that housed the Suburban. He bent down and grabbed the bottom corner of one of the large doors and pulled. A space opened up that was about six inches wide. He looked up at the doors and saw that they were probably locked from the inside.

Just then a flash of lightning lit up the night. It was followed a few seconds later by a low rumble of thunder. In a flash, the dog darted through the gap in the doors and disappeared inside.

"Not again," Dean said as the first few raindrops stabbed down at the boys. "Now we *have* to get inside."

"That's where you can help," Andrew said. "You're the smallest, so I'll need you to get down on your hands and knees. We're going to heave on the bottom corner of this door and try and open up enough space for you to crawl through."

"You want *me* to crawl in *there*?" Dean asked. "What if there's bats inside?"

"There won't be," Andrew said. "There's no way the owner would risk having them poop on his truck."

"True enough," Dean said. He got down on his hands and knees in front of the doors. The dog peeked out and licked his face and then ducked back inside.

"Yuck!" Dean grimaced as he wiped the slobber from

his nose. He couldn't help but smile though. He glanced up at Andrew and nodded. "Ready."

Matt and Chad got into position with Andrew, and together, the three boys heaved on the doors.

"Is it wide enough?" Andrew asked, grunting through clenched teeth. The rain was falling harder now. The boys heard it hitting the ground all around them. Another rumble of thunder sounded in the distance, and the dog let out a howl.

"Almost," Dean said. "Another few centimeters. Just don't let go of it on my head!"

Straining with exertion, the boys gave the door another heave and managed to pull it out a bit more.

"Careful we don't bend the door!" Andrew warned.

"I think that's wide enough," Dean said. He stuck his head inside, turned his shoulders sideways, and then wriggled through the gap. "I'm in!"

"Can you unlock the doors?" Andrew asked.

"Not these ones, they're chained shut."

"How about the side door?" Andrew asked.

No answer.

Then a scream.

"Dean!" Matt shouted. "Are you okay?"

Another scream. It sounded like it came from deeper in the building.

"Help me!" Dean cried.

Andrew grabbed the corner of the door. "Come on, guys, pull!"

They boys heaved on the door with all their might.

"Matt, do you think you can make it inside if Chad and I pull?"

"I don't know!"

"Try!"

"Hey guys, what's all the fuss about?"

The boys all looked up at Dean, who had just sauntered around the side of the building.

Matt's shocked face burst into a smile. "Why you—"

"Gotcha!"

Dean broke into a fit of laughter. The other boys weren't far behind.

"Oh man," Dean said when he finally caught his breath. "You should have seen the look on your faces."

"So you got the door unlocked?" Matt asked.

"No, I discovered a transporter inside from *Star Trek* and beamed my way out. Of course I got it open. Come on."

He led the boys around to the side door and pushed it open. "Welcome to my Casbah," Dean said as he stepped aside and ushered the boys in.

The boys filed inside, and Dean shut the door behind them. They had to squeeze past the Suburban, which just barely fit inside the garage.

"Boy, it sure is great to get out of that wind and rain," Matt said as he rubbed his arms. "Now what?" He looked down at the floor. "Not much room to sit, never mind lie down."

Andrew shone Dean's flashlight around the shed. He walked over to the driver's side of the truck and shone the light in the window. His eyes lit up. "You are not going to believe this."

"What?" Matt asked.

In reply, Andrew grabbed the Suburban's door handle and opened it. The shed was filled with a burst of light from the vehicle's interior lamp as well as a dinging sound.

Andrew leaned inside. "The keys are in the ignition. Can you believe that? They chain the doors shut, but they leave the keys in the ignition!"

"Must have forgotten them," Chad said. "Maybe they left in a hurry."

Andrew nodded. "Maybe." He got in and sat down in

the driver's seat.

"Let's start it up," Matt said as he went around to the passenger's side. "Get some heat going."

"Are you kidding? We'd all suffocate from the fumes," Dean said.

"Even if we opened the side door?" Matt asked.

"I wouldn't want to risk it," Andrew said as Matt opened the passenger door. Matt was about to get in when Andrew stopped him. "Take your muddy shoes off. We don't want to get it dirty. And take off anything else that might muck it up. I think we can spend the night in here, but I don't want to wreck their vehicle doing it."

"I don't know, guys, what if they come home?" Dean asked.

"Then we'll tell them what happened, that we were freezing," Matt said.

"Don't worry, Dean, I'm sure they'll understand," Chad assured his friend. "Come on."

"Okay." Dean stretched and sighed. "It sure beats sleeping on the ground."

Just then another peal of thunder rumbled, and the dog nosed Dean's leg. Dean scratched the dog's head and then looked up.

"Hey, what about him?"

"He definitely stays outside," Andrew said.

"In the storm?"

"Yup."

"Can't he at least stay in the garage?"

Andrew looked around the building and shrugged. "I don't see why not."

Dean looked down at the dog. "Sorry, boy. At least you get to stay inside here, away from the rain." Just then, another rumble shook the shed. "And the thunder."

The boys took off their dirty shoes and outer clothing and then climbed into the truck, excited to be back in somewhat more "civilized" surroundings.

"Hey, Andrew, turn on the radio," Matt said. "Maybe there's something on there about us."

"I sure hope not," Chad said.

"Me, too," Dean agreed. "If we're on the radio, that means our parents are really spooked."

Andrew turned the keys to "accessory," and Matt tuned in the local radio station. It was in the middle of a sad country song. The boys weren't normally into country music, but they listened eagerly to the sound, thankful to hear a voice from the outside world. They hadn't realized how isolated they felt until that moment, even though they had only been gone a day.

After the song ended, the announcer came back on. He gave the weather forecast and then promised to give the news in a few minutes. The boys listened through a few ads until the announcer returned. They listened carefully to each news story, but there was nothing about them. The boys relaxed somewhat. Matt was just about to turn off the radio when Chad stopped him.

"Wait, they're going to update us on the game."

They listened as the announcer stated the Calgary Flames were up on the Edmonton Oilers 3-0 in the first period.

"What?" Chad exclaimed. "They're never going to dig themselves out of that hole. I'm glad I didn't watch it."

"Can I turn the radio off now?" Andrew asked.

"Go ahead," Chad said.

The boys stretched out on the Suburban's leather seats. Chad and Dean each got their own bench seat to themselves. Andrew and Matt reclined the two front seats until they were almost lying flat.

"Man, this feels good," Matt said as he wriggled to find a more comfortable position. "I'm still a little cold, though. Must be these wet socks." He bent down and peeled them off.

Chad yawned. "What time is it, Andrew?"

"Seven thirty," Andrew replied, his eyes already closed. The sound of the rain drumming on the garage roof was soothing.

"Wow, this is when my little sister goes to bed," Dean said with a yawn.

Moments later, the vehicle was filled with the sound of snoring.

"Dean!" Matt said groggily as he rolled over onto his side. The snoring continued.

"Reach over and give him a poke, would you, Chad?" Matt asked.

Chad raised himself up on one elbow and shook Dean's shoulder. Dean frowned, muttered something in his sleep, and then turned over. The snoring ceased, and within minutes, all four boys were fast asleep.

13

THE FINAL LEG

The boys awoke to the sound of paws scratching on wood. Matt was the first to stir. He opened his bleary eyes to the sight of the Suburban's gray interior and had to think for a few moments before he remembered where he was.

He sat up slowly and rubbed his neck, which was stiff from shivering and from lying at an awkward angle all night. He leaned forward and peered through the windshield. The dog was standing at the side door. It looked at Matt expectantly, its tail wagging excitedly, and then scratched the door again. Suddenly, Matt realized his own need to step outside and quickly got out of the truck. The sound of the door slamming awoke the other guys, and soon everyone was stirring.

Matt stumbled around the front of the Suburban and opened the side door. The dog was off like a shot and disappeared into some short bushes nearby to do his business. Matt quickly put on his shoes and coat and did the same.

When he was finished, he looked out at the sky, which was slowly coming to life with the rising sun. The air was crisp and cool, and the grass was soaked with the previous night's rain. Matt couldn't shake the chill, but it still felt good to be outside at dawn. He realized he had rarely been up early enough to see the sunrise, and he thought he would stand and wait for it, cold or not.

A few moments later, the garage door opened, and the other guys stumbled out. First Andrew, then Chad, and then Dean. They rubbed their eyes, and their hair stuck out in all directions as they came to stand by Matt. Even the dog came bounding up. It headed straight for Dean and licked his hand. Dean was happy to greet his new friend.

"It's amazing, isn't it?" Matt said.

"What's amazing?" Chad asked.

"That." Matt pointed up at the clouds, which were stretched out in thick, jagged strips across the sky, as if they had been painted with a brush. They were just starting to turn from gray to purple to red as the sun peeked over the horizon.

"Red sky at morning, sailor's warning," Andrew said. Right on cue, a breeze ruffled their hair.

"Yikes," Dean said. "What does that mean?"

"Bad weather coming," Andrew replied.

Dean groaned. "Great."

"Well, guess we'd better get moving then," Matt said. He rubbed his stomach. "I sure wish we had saved some food for breakfast."

"Me, too," Chad agreed. "But I guess the sooner we get moving, the sooner we get home—and the sooner we can see what's in the fridge."

"If our parents haven't put a padlock on it by then," Dean said.

That stopped the conversation dead as the boys all realized what the remainder of the day held for them when—or if—they got home. None of them were looking forward to facing their parents.

"Maybe they'll be so glad to see us they'll forget to be angry," Matt said.

"Not mine," Dean replied.

"Mine either," Andrew said.

Matt smiled. "I know exactly what our parents are going to say, hey Chad?"

"How can two smart boys be so stupid?" the brothers said in unison.

"That's about the size of it," Andrew said. "Shall we get going?"

"I just have to grab my pack," Dean said.

He ran back inside the garage, made sure everything was the way they found it in the Suburban, and then relocked the shed door and came out. The other boys were already starting down the hill, and Dean had to jog to catch up. The dog jumped and spun around in the air as he kept pace with Dean.

When the boys made their way down to the shore, they discovered the water was just beginning to lap at the back end of their canoes.

"That's funny," Matt said. "I was sure we pulled them completely out of the water last night."

"Do you think the water level could have risen that much?" Chad asked, turning to Andrew.

"I suppose so," Andrew said. "It must have. Probably because of the rain. I'm sure it's peaked by now though."

"We'd better get moving before it all drains away then," Matt said. He stepped forward and turned over the canoe. "Good thing you had us stow our things underneath, Andrew."

"It'll take a couple of days for the water to fall back again," Andrew said. "We could probably paddle around out here for a week before we got stranded."

"Well, I don't want to wait around that long to find

out," Dean said. "Let's get moving."

The boys decided to follow the shoreline to the east, where Chad had spotted the grain bins the evening before. There was no guarantee anyone lived around there, but they didn't know where else to go.

"Goodbye, boy," Dean said as he hugged the dog. "Hope your owners come home soon." The dog seemed to know it wasn't going on the trip. It didn't even try to get into Dean's canoe.

"We'll have to come back here sometime once the flood is over," Matt said. "I'm curious to see what this place looks like without all the water. I'm sure the pasture manager would be interested in hearing our story as well."

"We'll leave out the part about the Suburban though," Chad said.

"Good idea," Matt replied.

The sky continued to lighten as the boys paddled away. They kept the canoes about ten meters out from shore so they could stay somewhat sheltered from the north wind, which was already beginning to pick up. They were thankful for the meager warmth offered by their life jackets.

About thirty minutes later, the boys sighted the grain bins. The three, fat, silver cylinders flashed in the early morning sun as it peeked in and out of a cloud bank. Encouraged that the bins were not just an illusion, the boys dug in their paddles and pulled hard toward their destination.

Twenty minutes later, they had halved the distance between them and the bins, and for the first time, they caught sight of a farmhouse just up the hill and to the right of the bins. A pick-up truck was parked to one side of the house, and there appeared to be a light in one of the windows, although it was difficult to tell if it was a light or merely the rising sun reflecting of the glass. Either way, the boys were excited by the discovery.

"I knew we should have kept going last night," Dean said.

"We had no way of knowing," Andrew replied. "Besides, it wouldn't have been safe to be on the water with all that lightning."

The boys saw a natural inlet at the base of the hill just to the right of the bins and below the house. They beached the canoes on a bed of close-cropped grass and then raced up the hill without even bothering to take off their life jackets. Everyone was anxious to discover whether or not they had finally reached the end of the trip, even though they knew they were in for trouble once they finally made it home.

Their curiosity was answered about halfway up the hill when they heard a tractor fire up. The old diesel engine coughed and sputtered before it roared to life, belching a huge ball of black smoke into the crisp morning air above the pair of low-slung cattle barns located just east of the house.

"Whoo-hoo!" Matt said, thankful that he finally had something to cheer about again.

The boys raced up the remaining part of the hill and carefully crossed a barbed wire fence that bordered a row of huge, drooping elm trees at the top of the hill. Dean snagged the back of his life jacket on the top strand of wire and had to get Andrew to help him get free.

"Come on, you guys!" Matt said, impatient to make contact with whoever lived at the farm.

Once Dean was free, the boys ducked and weaved through the elm trees and emerged into the farmyard just as the tractor rounded the corner of the barn, a round straw bale impaled on two spikes that jutted out of the bucket of its front-end loader. The farmer was probably on his way to lay it down for bedding for the small herd of cattle located in a corral just behind the barns.

The farmer did not see the boys at first. Then he glanced toward them, did a double take, and his mouth fell open in surprise. He scrambled to stop the tractor before he drove straight into the barn. Then he jammed the machine into neutral, stepped on the emergency brake, and jumped down and walked over to the boys.

The boys rushed forward, anxious to talk to the first person outside their group that they had seen in the past twenty-four hours.

The farmer had a stern look on his face as he approached, and the boys slowed down somewhat, fearful he was going to accuse them of trespassing. They stopped within a few meters of him and then stood there meekly as he looked them up and down.

"What on earth?" the farmer exclaimed.

He took in their tired faces, tousled hair, and bright orange life jackets, and then he let out a hoot of laughter. The boys grinned sheepishly, not knowing what to say. He looked away from the boys and then turned back, slapped his knee, and broke out into another laugh.

"Is this some kind of a joke? Where did you all come from?"

Matt pointed down the hill behind them. He started to speak, but then had to clear his throat, because it was so dry. "Down the hill there, sir. In the water."

The farmer stepped past the boys and spotted the canoes. He turned back to the boys and looked at his watch. "You're up awful early. When did you start out?"

"Yesterday," Andrew said. "Yesterday morning, actually."

"From where?" the farmer asked, his face melting into a frown.

"Milligan Creek."

The farmer glanced toward the town, the lights of which glistened in the distance. "That's six miles from here!"

Andrew nodded. "We know."

"Boy, do we know it," Matt added.

Led by Matt, the boys launched into their tale, recounting how they had disobeyed their parents and gone farther than they were supposed to in order to get Andrew's paddle and then lost their way in the flood plain. The farmer laughed at certain spots, shook his head at others, then finally held up his hand for them to stop.

"Just let me turn off my tractor, and we'll go inside. You boys must be freezing. You had any breakfast?"

They shook their heads.

"Well, my wife should just about have it on by now. We'll go inside and see. Then you can phone your parents and tell them you're all right. I'm Albert Brown, by the way." He shook hands with each of them in turn as the boys told him their names.

"Matt and Chad Taylor?" Albert said when he got to them. "Your dad the one with the spray plane?"

They nodded.

"I know him well enough." Albert smiled. "Now I've definitely got something to talk about next time I see him."

Matt and Chad stared at the ground with grins on their reddening faces.

The boys waited while Albert shut down his tractor. Then they followed him toward the house. It was a simple, two-story affair. It needed some paint and a few other touch-ups on the outside, but the boys did not care. They were just thankful to be someplace warm and dry.

The smell of oatmeal porridge and coffee met them as they entered the kitchen. Porridge wasn't something they normally liked to eat, but at that moment, it smelled marvelous.

"Look what I have here," Albert said as he entered.

His wife turned from where she had been stirring the porridge at the stove. She nearly dropped her wooden spoon in surprise at the sight of the boys. "What the heck?"

A young boy—about two years old—clung to her legs and peeked out at the boys from between her knees. Chad winked at the boy, who ducked out of sight.

"Voyagers, I think you'd call them," Albert said and laughed. "You can take off your life jackets now, boys. I don't think there's a chance of us sinking in this flood. Better put on some more porridge, Lynda."

"Don't mind him," Lynda said as the boys took off their life jackets and shoes. "I'm sure you've already told Albert, but now I want you to tell me how you ended up in our yard at six thirty in the morning with life jackets on. But first, sit down, and we'll get some hot food into you. Albert, you're going to have to wait for the second batch."

"Fair enough," Albert said. "I'll go and drop that bale off and be right back."

After Albert left, Andrew turned to Lynda. "I don't mean to be a pain, but is there anywhere we can wash up?" he asked. "We're pretty filthy."

"Of course." She showed them to the bathroom, which was located just off the kitchen. "Here are some old towels and washcloths." She opened a cupboard and pulled them out. "Feel free to muck them up. They're the ones Albert uses when he's all dirty from working in the barns."

"Thanks, Mrs. Brown," Chad said.

After the boys finished washing up, they took a seat around the table. Lynda had already spooned out a bowl of porridge for each of them. They piled on some brown sugar and raisins and then drowned it in milk. Before long, they were all digging into the steaming breakfast. As they ate, they recounted their tale for Lynda. She laughed at some of the things they had done and experienced. When it was all over, she shook her head.

"Well, I have never heard of anyone shooting down Milligan Creek like that. You boys should tell your story to the paper."

"We might not have a choice," Matt said. "They already took our picture as we passed through town. They'll probably want to do a follow-up story when they find out what happened."

Albert came in as the boys were finishing their breakfast. "So, you guys all fed up now?"

"Yes, Mr. Brown, thanks," Andrew said.

"Sure killed my appetite," Matt quipped.

The other boys groaned at his lame joke.

"Well, I suppose you'll be wanting to phone your parents now." Albert pointed to a black phone that was hanging on the wall beside the doorway that led to their living room. "Feel free to use it."

The boys looked at each other.

"Anyone want to go first?" Matt asked.

"I vote for you," Dean said. "You're the one who got us into this mess."

"Hey, I've got an idea," Matt said, "why don't we phone each other's parents? That way they can't get so mad at us."

"My mom will have no problem getting angry at you, Matt," Dean said.

"Good point," Matt replied. He took a deep breath and then let it out. "Well, I guess it's now or never." He walked over to the phone, took another deep breath, and then dialed.

"Hello, Mom?" he said a few moments later. He pulled the receiver away from his ear for a moment, grimacing, and then held it back to his ear. "Yes, it's Matt. Chad's right here with me. So are Dean and Andrew." He listened for a moment. "Yes, yes, we're all right." He listened again. "We just got a little lost. No, not in town, past town, just a little bit." He glanced back to the boys and grimaced.

"It's not going well," Dean whispered.

"Yes, I know we disobeyed. I'm sorry," Matt said. "We're at Albert and Lynda Brown's place. That's right, on the north edge of the community pasture. Half an hour? Sounds good."

"Wait a minute," Albert interjected.

"Just a second, Mom." Matt put his hand over the phone.

"There's no need for them to come all the way out here," Albert said. "I was about to head into town anyway. Why don't we just throw the canoes into the back of the truck, and I'll drive you into town?"

Matt looked at the other boys. They all nodded. Things would go better for them if their parents were inconvenienced as little as possible. Matt put the phone back to his ear.

"Actually, Mom, Mr. Brown said he'd drive us in. No, it's no problem. He was going into town anyway. Okay, we'll meet you at Dean's. And Mom, we're really sorry. Okay, goodbye."

He hung up the phone and stared at it.

"Well, how'd she sound?" Dean asked.

"Don't worry, Dean. She's phoning your mom for you—your mom, too, Andrew. I guess they were up half the night searching for us. Dad's plane is having some mechanical troubles, which is why they didn't use it in the search."

"Oh no." Dean sank into his chair. He looked over at Albert. "Can we start loading up now? I just want to get this over with."

"Whenever you're ready," Albert said, standing up.

"Thank you so much for breakfast, Mrs. Brown," Matt said.

"Yeah, thanks," the other guys echoed.

"Don't mention it," Lynda answered, chuckling. "And I hope everything goes well with your parents. Don't worry, they'll get over it."

"Yeah, but will we?" Dean asked.

"No matter what happens, you boys have got a great story!" Lynda chuckled again as she ushered the boys out of the house.

The boys had a hard time sharing in her good cheer.

14

Day of Reckoning

Albert turned left off the gravel road and onto Highway 310. The truck rumbled as he ran through the gears and got it up to speed. The boys watched the landscape keenly as they sped along, looking for any sign of the route they had just traveled. As they neared town, Albert glanced back at Dean.

"Where'd you say your house was?" he asked.

"On the north side of the tracks, just off Broadway," Dean replied. "You can turn left up there if you want. Take the road past the graveyard."

"Will do," Albert said as he geared down. He waited for another car to pass in the opposite lane and then turned left onto the gravel road. It curved around a banked corner and then dipped down toward the creek. As they drew up to the graveyard bridge, the boys couldn't believe their eyes. The bridge deck was completely gone. Only the metal frame remained. The town works crew was in the midst of cordoning off the area with orange pylons and barriers.

"Washed out!" Matt exclaimed. "So the water really did rise last night."

Albert nodded. "It sure was a fast melt. Never seen

anything like it." The boys stared in awe for a few seconds at the spot where the bridge used to be. Then Albert put the truck into reverse and backed up the hill until he came to a driveway. He turned around and headed back the way they had come.

Within a few minutes, the boys passed through town, crossed the tracks, and turned onto Broadway. As they pulled up to Dean's house, they saw the Taylors and Loewens were already there.

"I guess this is it," Matt said as Albert came to a stop.

"Good luck, boys," Albert said. "Look on the bright side: Like Lynda said, you've got some story to tell."

"Thanks," Chad replied. "And thanks for everything you've done for us."

"Don't mention it," Albert said. "Stop by again next year if you like. But be sure to call first so we know to have breakfast on!" He laughed heartily.

"Funny," Matt said. "Real funny."

The boys took a deep breath, and then Andrew opened the door and stepped out. Matt followed him. Then came Chad and finally Dean.

The moment all four boys were outside; they were blinded by a camera flash.

"What's that all about?" Matt said, holding up his hand to block the glare.

"Who knows? This may be the last picture we ever get of you—alive!" Joyce said from behind the camera.

"That's what you said yesterday," Matt muttered.

"This time I mean it," she replied. "Smile!" She snapped another picture. "You guys are in *huge* trouble," she whispered.

"Thanks, Joyce," Matt said, scowling.

The boys waited quietly as their parents walked over from where they had been talking in the Mullers' driveway. The men went over to help Albert unload the canoes and then thanked him for his help. Albert honked as he pulled away, and the boys all turned to wave. Then they turned back to their parents, hung their heads, and waited for the barrage they knew was coming.

"So, the adventurers return," Mr. Taylor said, putting his hands on his hips. "Anyone care to tell us whose crazy idea it was to go past the graveyard bridge?"

The boys were all silent, but one by one they all turned to Matt.

"Okay, it was me," he said. "But it was an accident. We were just going after Andrew's paddle, and by the time we got it, there was no way to turn back."

"What?" Mr. Loewen asked. "How did Andrew lose his paddle?"

"When we capsized," Andrew said.

"Capsized?" Mrs. Muller cried. "Dean, are you all right?" She rushed forward to look him over.

"Yes, Mom, of course." He glanced nervously at Joyce.

"It was only Andrew and me," Matt said. "We got caught in some rapids and slammed right into a big tree that was hanging over the water. Andrew went under, and the canoe tipped right over and sank."

"Oh my Lord," Mrs. Muller said, putting her hand to her chest.

"Chad and I didn't shoot the rapids," Dean said. He smiled weakly, hoping his mother would be impressed with his caution. She glared at him until his smile faded away. He turned toward Joyce instead.

"Chad and I *portaged* around the rapids," he said, emphasizing the word in the hopes of impressing her with his expanding vocabulary.

Joyce appeared unmoved.

"Dean J. Muller!"

Dean turned back quickly to face his mother. "Yes, Mom?"

"Come here!"

Dean glanced back at the guys and then stepped forward. A second later, his mom grabbed him in a huge hug.

"I thought you were dead!"

"No, Mom, I'm okay, really," Dean said. He glanced over at Joyce and tried to pull back. "Really, it was a great trip. We saw a deer, visited an old farmyard, and I even met a really cool dog. It was wild, right guys?"

The other boys nodded quickly, sensing an opportunity to gain some ground.

"Yeah, and Mrs. Muller, we couldn't have made it without Dean and all that stuff you packed for him. I don't know what we would have done without it."

Mrs. Muller scowled at Matt and then turned back to Dean and gave him another squeeze. "Hmph."

Mr. Loewen tilted his cap back and rubbed his forehead. "Well, I can imagine you guys are exhausted, probably haven't had much sleep. By the way, where did you sleep last night? That was quite the storm."

The boys looked at each other and grinned. "In a Suburban," Andrew said.

Mr. Loewen frowned. "Huh?"

"It's a long story," Matt said.

"Why don't we talk about it over breakfast?" Mr. Taylor suggested. "Our treat."

"Sounds great," Mrs. Taylor agreed. "We can talk about punishments, too." She glared at each of the boys and then turned back to the adults. "Is Wendy's Grill okay with everyone?"

The Mullers and Loewens agreed, and they all moved toward their vehicles.

"One more thing before we go," Mr. Muller said, turning to face the rest of the boys. "Andrew, Matt, Dean, Chad, how can such smart boys like you—"

"Be so stupid?" the boys replied.

"Exactly."

The boys looked at each other and grinned.

Matt turned back to Mr. Muller, barely able to contain the laughter that was bubbling up in his throat. "Don't worry, Mr. Muller. We won't make the same mistake next year."

Mr. Muller scowled. "Next year?"

"You'll still be grounded next year, Matt Taylor," Matt's mother said.

"Aw, Mom,"

"Just get in the truck," she said, grabbing Matt and Chad around the neck and giving them a hug. "Two years from now, maybe. But next year? Out of the question."

"Come on, six months?" Matt said as headed toward the truck.

Mr. Taylor pointed his finger at his son. "Don't push it! You're not even *in* the doghouse yet, much less out of it."

"And once you're out of his doghouse, it's straight into mine, Matt Taylor!" Mrs. Muller said.

She tried to keep a straight face, but then she started to chuckle despite herself.

"Aw, get over here." She gave him a big hug. "I'm just happy you're safe. All of you—including you, Matt."

The boys laughed as they climbed into their parents' vehicles, thankful to be home, thankful that the confrontation was over—almost—and already looking forward to their *next* adventure.

UNLIMITED

A school field trip to the local Wetlands Unlimited marsh just outside Milligan Creek gives Matt, Chad, Dean, and Andrew a brilliant idea: hijacking the radio signal that broadcasts a recorded message about the marsh and using it to launch their own pirate radio station. Broadcasting late at night, mostly for their own amusement, their show quickly becomes an underground sensation. Keeping their identities a secret, the boys are ecstatic about the growing popularity of their program, until it draws the attention of Wetlands Unlimited—and the police!

THE WATER WAR

Another long, hot, boring summer has the guys wondering how to fill their time. Then they come up with the perfect plan: a "water war," the ultimate game of survival, where every kid in town is simultaneously hunter and prey. With everyone a potential enemy, even Matt, Chad, Dean, and Andrew's friendship is put to the test. As the summer draws to a close and participants keep dropping like flies, only one question remains: who will be the last person standing?

For more details on these books and other titles in the Milligan Creek series, please visit www.millstonepress.ca or www.facebook.com/MilliganCreekSeries.

About the Author

Kevin Miller grew up on a farm outside of Foam Lake, Saskatchewan, where he dreamed of becoming a writer. He got his first break as a newspaper reporter in Meadow Lake, SK. Within a year, he parlayed that into a job in book publishing, which eventually enabled him to become a full-time freelance writer and editor.

From there, Kevin transitioned into film, and he spent the next ten years traveling the world while working on a variety of feature films, documentaries, and short film projects. In addition to serving as a writer, he has also worked as a director, producer, and film editor.

These days, Kevin splits his time between film and book publishing, and he also does a bit of teaching on the side. In his spare time, he enjoys hanging out with his wife and four kids, fishing, hiking, canoeing (of course), skiing, skateboarding, and otherwise exploring his world.

Kevin likes to talk about books, movies, and writing almost as much as he enjoys writing itself. If you'd like to contact Kevin about any of these topics, to tell him what you think of this novel, or to book him for a speaking engagement, you can reach him at www.millstonepress.ca or www.facebook.com/MilliganCreekSeries.

13594930R00080

Made in the USA
San Bernardino, CA
22 December 2018